Little
One

Kieran Brookes

SRL Publishing Ltd

SRL Publishing Ltd
Office 47396, PO Box 6945
London
W1A 6US

First published worldwide by SRL Publishing in 2021

ISBN: 978-1-8382798-0-6

This book was written during quarantine, 2020, and I'd like to dedicate it to the doctors, nurses, healthcare professionals, and all the other frontline workers who put their own lives on the line, during this most trying of times, to help others.

I'd also like to dedicate it to Ramon Thompson. Rest in Peace, Granddad. We miss you...

Gwendolyn Anne Becker, beloved mother to Claire Elaine Becker and Noah Matthew Becker, and husband to the late Frank Alexander Becker, passed away at her family home in Neilston (the exact date of her passing has yet to be confirmed). A long-time resident of Neilston, Gwendolyn was beloved by many and will be dearly missed by her children, Claire and Noah. A small service has been arranged for Saturday 27th August, at Our Lady of Sorrows Church, in Neilston. Proceedings will begin at 12pm.

Claire Elaine Becker, 28, beloved daughter of Gwendolyn Anne Becker and Frank Alexander Becker, passed away suddenly on Tuesday, 18th August, following an accident on the road between Grandtully and Aberfeldy, in northern Perthshire. Claire was the eldest child of Gwendolyn and Frank and leaves behind her younger brother, Noah. At the request of her brother, Claire is to be laid to rest on the same day as their mother, who sadly passed away in the weeks prior to Claire's passing. Both women will be laid to rest beside the late Frank Alexander Becker, in Neilston Cemetery, on Saturday 27th August. A brief service will be held at the Our Lady of Sorrows Church at 12pm on the day.

Noah Matthew Becker, born 16th April, 1983, passed away on Friday, 21st August, following an incident at the High Court of Judiciary in Glasgow. He will now be laid to rest on the same day as his sister, Claire Elaine Becker, who sadly passed away three days prior to Noah's passing, and his mother, Gwendolyn Anne Becker, who also passed recently. Claire and Noah were the only children of Gwendolyn and Frank Becker (both now deceased). The joint service will be held on Saturday, 27th August, at Our Lady of Sorrows Church, in Neilston. Proceedings will begin at 12pm.

Prologue
Adam Hunt

Of all the possible ways his life could have gone, Adam could not have believed, in his wildest most fantastical dreams, the sequence of events that he'd just watched unfold over the past eight weeks. The Judge, or Lord Justice, or Lord President, or whatever you wanted to call him, had just thrown the book at him in the most damning way possible; sealing his fate, erasing his future and topping off what had been, without a doubt, the worst two months of his life. Eighteen years at HMP Deepwood and now he had all the time in the world to mull it over.

Deepwood was situated in Brackletter, not far from Fort William in the Highlands of Scotland. The River Spean ran nearby and General Wade's military road, between Fort William and Fort Augustus, was only a short walking distance away. Adam had walked that road with his father as a boy; the old military roads of Scotland had always fascinated Jack Hunt. Constructed during the middle parts of the eighteenth century in a vain attempt by the Government to bring order to a region in turmoil, after the Jacobite Rebellion of 1715; Adam had been bored to tears as his father recounted these endless titbits to him on their long country walks together.

The site where Deepwood now stood was famous for the one night in June, 1941, during the second Great War, when it housed the now notorious Nazi war criminal, Rudolph Hess, before his transfer to the Tower of London the next day. In 1941, Deepwood had been a barracks for the Royal Observer Corps and was intended to be a holding place for Hess until the war came to an end. The barracks were converted to a prison in the mid-1960s, and the building in which Hess had slept was knocked down in the 1980s during renovations to the East Wing. The sole remnant of his stay is a small plaque marking the spot that had once been his cell.

Adam reflected on these shadows from the past as they travelled. This part of Scotland saw nothing but snow for five months of the year, while the skiing season flourished, then the next seven months were nothing but rain. It battered the tiny windows of the G4S custodial truck, as it wound along the backroads on its way north through the Highlands, from Glasgow High Court of Justiciary; a granite essay in neo-classicism that glares over the banks of the River Clyde.

It was a three-hour drive through a beautiful stretch of country. Not that Adam could see any of it; the narrow windows of the custodial truck were barely eight inches wide and the plastic was frosted and pockmarked with graffiti. Prisoners weren't meant to be able to enjoy the view on rides like this, and passers-by weren't meant to be able to see inside either. Incidentally, Adam's fellow passengers were some of the lewdest and most violent looking men that he'd ever had the displeasure to lay eyes on, and the screws at G4S Custodial preferred to spare the public's eyes the same misfortune.

Inside the truck, each prisoner was squeezed inside their own tiny compartment. They offered little to no cushioning when the truck lurched cruelly, throwing Adam hard against the wall. In essence, it wasn't a seat that Adam sat on as much as it was a bench, and seatbelts, of course, were a needless expenditure in such vehicles. The compartment had been designed to allow for as little room as possible; his knees were pressed painfully against the plastic wall in front of him, locking him into a fully upright position. Only the top half of his body remained free to roam the cabin. His wrists lay handcuffed between his thighs and other than the foot or so of space above his head, he had absolutely no room to manoeuvre himself.

Adam would come to learn that these trucks, amongst the community of convicts, were lovingly referred to as '*sweat boxes*'; but the way he remembered that first trip, '*ice-boxes*' would have been a more fitting moniker. It was the most claustrophobic situation he'd ever found himself in, and he tried not to think about it as the truck ploughed ceaselessly through the rain. That three-hour drive up to Deepwood had felt like an eternity. He couldn't wait for it to be over. Adam didn't know it at the time, but a few days from now he would gladly have spent an eternity in that truck if it got him away from Deepwood.

While on remand, he'd managed to get a hold of a copy of the Scottish Daily Telegraph, featuring himself on the front page. They'd used a picture of him from his wedding day, alongside his bride – '*Perth Man Arrested on Suspicion of Murder*', read the title. Although the picture was flattering, the article was not.

Police have arrested a twenty-five-year-old man in connection with the death of his wife. The woman, twenty-six, was found with knife wounds to her neck; medics at the scene were unable to revive her. She was pronounced dead shortly thereafter.

When asked for comment, Constable Alan McDonald, of Perth and Kinross Police, had the following to say:

'We've taken a man into custody who we believe has information regarding the incident in question.'

When asked about a motive, Constable McDonald replied:

'We have no clear motive at present, but questioning is underway, and we are confident of charging a suspect within the next 24 hours.'

If charged, the accused will likely spend the next twenty to thirty years behind bars. Until then, residents are left wondering why yet another murder has shaken the once peaceful City of Perth.

Chapter 1
Claire

Claire rolled over and slammed the snooze button on the Remington clock radio alarm that was an old gift from her brother. It was Wednesday, 6am, and Wednesday was a school day. She'd been subbing at St George's for nearly six months now and the days didn't seem to be getting any shorter. Why she'd assumed a class full of nine-year-olds would be preferable to long days in a courtroom, sat beside the world's most despicable miscreants, was beyond her.

Defending criminals hadn't exactly been the glitz and the glamour she'd been hoping a career in law would bring her. Especially in London, where knife-crime was rife, and the hope of a viable defence was essentially non-existent. Her job had been reduced to escorting her clients from their brief day in court, straight back to the holding cells where they came from. In essence, she'd been reduced to a middleman - a boatman for the damned, ferrying them across the long winding judicial system to the Underworld - though she would never admit that to herself. These men didn't belong out on the streets: Thieves, rapists, murderers... even terrorists; London was brimming with the lot of them. The ones with enough money to afford legal representation from a firm such as her own were only delaying the inevitable.

Claire had fallen into the world of criminal law in much the saw way most studious, bright-eyed overachievers did. She'd grown up watching Ally McBeal on Channel 4 in the evenings with her mother and decided right there and then, at fifteen-years-old, that that's what she was going to do with her life. She certainly had the brains for it (plus her mother's brother, Duncan, had been a lawyer in his day, so it kind of ran in the family).

After acing her A-levels in high school then graduating with a first-class degree in Law from the University of Westminster, she'd landed her dream job a month later in the centre of one of the most exciting cities in the world. Dean, Whitney and Campbell LLP had hired her as one of their graduate legal assistants at their offices on Tottenham Court Road. After two years of shadowing one of the more senior solicitors, and after studying for more professional exams than she cared to remember, she was ready to take on her own cases.

The first person who arrived at her desk, for her very first case, was a man named Asif Hussain. He'd been making rounds on the news stations recently as one of the four terrorists responsible for the Boxing Day bombings that shook the country in the winter of 2005. Unfortunately for Asif, the suicide vest which he'd intended to end his own life with, as well as the lives of countless others on the bus that day, had served only to sever his right arm and puncture his right lung. The vest had misfired and only partially detonated, maiming Asif and badly injuring seven other people in the process. After six months in a hospital and six months detained in a prison cell at Pentonville, he was finally declared suitable to stand trial for his intended crimes against the people of the West.

Fortunately for Hussain (who now wore a suit with one empty arm pinned up at the elbow), his father had sourced him the necessary funds to procure the council of Dean, Whitney and Campbell (not the most expensive firm on the block by any means, but far from the cheapest). The Partners had decided, with their all-knowing wisdom, to pass this case on to one of their newly promoted junior solicitors. Thus, it was Claire's office door that Mr Hussain's father would walk through on that rainy Monday morning back in December 2006.

The visits to the prison in those months had been the scariest of her life. She'd visited prisons before, of course, during her shadowing days as a graduate trainee, but she'd always felt protected then, as if she were behind an invisible glass window; merely observing and thus impervious to harm. Now she was out on her own, she felt more vulnerable than she could ever have thought possible. They say you develop a thick skin working in the criminal justice system, but back in those days, Claire's skin was as translucent as her favourite drink, which happened to be vodka.

Asif's father had travelled down from Leeds, in the North East of England, where he owned and worked in a local corner shop with his wife Naila. Of his four children, Asif was the youngest at twenty years old. Asif's older sisters had both returned to Pakistan where they'd found husbands and started families of their own. Asif's brother, Imran, had a flat in the Beeston area of Leeds, and it was in this flat that Asif was living at the time of the bombing.

Asif had been a quiet boy growing up in Holbeck, near Leeds. His teachers had called him a 'slow gentle giant', due to his size and good nature. At school he had a good attendance record and did moderately well with his studies. According to his father, his problems began while at college, where he met Mohammed Abdul Khan and Shehzad Ali, with whom he frequented the Stratford Street mosque. He also became intimately associated with the Hamara Youth Access Point (a drop-in centre for teens) which was operated by the Hamara Healthy Living Centre – an Islamic charity partly funded by the UK government. It was at the Hamara Access Point that Asif's father believes he became intimately associated with radical individuals who put Asif on the path to destruction.

On the morning of December 26th, 2005, Asif, and three other Islamic terrorists, separately detonated three homemade devices in rapid succession aboard London Underground trains across the city. Then later, a fourth device was detonated by Asif himself aboard a double decker bus in Tavistock Square, in the London borough of Camden. Of the four bombers, Asif was the only one to survive. His right arm was completely severed by the blast from his vest, breaking seven of his ribs and puncturing his lung. As well as Asif's fellow attackers, fifty-two people died and over seven hundred were injured that day, resulting in one of the single biggest tragedies to happen on British soil since the bombing of Pan Am Flight 103 over Lockerby in Scotland. On the day that Asif Hussain's father walked into her office, Claire started the beginning of the end of her short but pivotal career in criminal law.

***

Three months after the trial of Asif Hussain had ended, and the media frenzy that had surrounded her for over a year had finally subsided, Claire quit her job at Dean, Whitney and Campbell, and hadn't looked back since (well, at least not until today). Since March this year, Claire had worked as a substitute teacher at St George the Martyr Church of England Primary School, in Camden. She taught mainly year fours, which were eight to nine years old, but occasionally taught some of the older kids in year five and year six. The teacher who Claire was substituting for, Mrs Higginbottom, had left on maternity leave and was due to extend her leave by a further three months owing to a suspected case of postpartum depression. This suited Claire just fine as it saved her the hassle of finding other travel arrangements for her next subby posting, wherever that may be.

St George's, as luck would have it, was walking distance from her flat in Camden - fifteen minutes walking distance to be precise. During this walk,

Claire passed King's Cross station every morning at precisely the same time. Today, as it was raining, she had her umbrella held high as she ploughed on through the crowd of pedestrians as they crossed the street towards the station. Battling with the wind, she reached in her pocket to grab a stick of chewing gum, before realising she was out of gum. To her left was a small newsstand which was thankfully queue-free. She rushed over to it, grabbing a packet of Wrigley's Tutti Frutti and handing it to the man seated opposite, hidden behind a somewhat imposing wall of chocolate bars. As the man handed Claire her change, she noticed the front page of one of the newspapers laying in a pile at her feet. The doubletake she did next was so violent that she brushed the entire front row of chocolate bars to the floor.

Picking them up clumsily and apologising, she couldn't take her eyes off the front page of that paper. Staring back at her from the wet, blurring ink of the Daily Telegraph was a face she hadn't seen in person for over a decade – the face of her increasingly estranged cousin, Adam.

Chapter 2
Once Upon a Time

Claire extracted the first paper from the pile and stared at the front page in mixed shock and disbelief. She recognised his face immediately. They had been close growing up, back in Scotland, until she'd moved down to London, just over a decade ago. Claire's father was his mother's older brother. They were cousins. Close cousins; well, at least until that Christmas in nineteen-ninety-seven …

Claire was just starting university and had found a small flat share in the Marylebone area of London. It was an utter dump, but she loved it, nonetheless. The independence it brought her, the freedom from her mother; she was liberated and she loved every second of it - even if the dirty dishes were piled as high as ant hills and she barely dared to open up her laundry hamper for the avalanche that might crush her.

That Christmas, Claire had travelled back home to spend the holidays with her family. Her parents' house in Neilston, just outside of Glasgow, was only a ninety-minute drive from her aunt and uncle's home in Perth.

Christmas had come and the whole family had settled under one roof in their recently refurbished attic-converted farmhouse on the outskirts of town. Claire was the most senior and responsible of the children (she was still classed as 'children' even though she was approaching her eighteenth birthday at the time). Next there was Adam, who was two years her junior, then Noah, her younger brother.

That evening, the festive music had been playing, the food had been plentiful, and the alcohol had been flowing in increasingly liberal measures. Claire wasn't much of a drinker (well at least not at that stage), but her parents and the other adults could quite easily have drunk a full-sized African elephant under the table. Each of them was uniquely intoxicated come eight o'clock that evening. Her father was the singer, dancing on the tables with a bottle of Morgan's Spiced in each hand; her mother was the denizen of sensibility - despite her vision of sensible becoming more and more obscure with each passing vodka; her aunt Molly always brought the emotion - brought to tears by waves of sentimentality, then in an instant she could be on her feet embroiled in the most heated of arguments; her uncle Jack was the joker, but come eleven-thirty that night, nobody was joking anymore.

From what Claire could remember, the drinks had started to run dry shortly before midnight and Frank had suggested taking a short trip in his car to the local off-licence, a mere five minutes' drive down the farm road. Claire agreed to stay at home and watch the kids while the four adults squeezed into her father's red Mondeo and puttered off down the road through the snow. The snow had been falling all week and there was at least a foot on the ground that night when it happened.

When they finally came back, nearly three hours later, it was approaching two in the morning and Claire, her brother and her cousin were all fast asleep in their beds. Claire woke up when she heard her father's car pull into the driveway. She listened as a brief argument broke out then quickly diminished; it was her father who was doing most of the talking. The front door opened, she heard two people step inside, then the door swiftly closed behind them. She heard raised voices again coming from outside – it was her uncle. Although Claire's bedroom had been on the ground floor and her room was the closest to the door, she could only catch snippets of what was being said.

'Are you sure about this? It just doesn't feel right, leaving them out there,' her uncle breathed heatedly.

'You promised – we don't have a choice,' her father replied.

Just then, the front door opened again, and the two men walked inside. Claire could still hear their voices as they stamped the snow from their boots and hung up their coats and wet gloves on the hooks by the door.

'Where did Molly go?'

'I'm not sure. Probably to bed.'

'Get up there and talk to her. You have to make sure she's not going to talk!'

'She won't. Don't worry.'

'We have to be sure. If anyone found out about this… well… just make sure she keeps her mouth shut, ok? I'll talk to Gwen…'

Claire heard the bolt on the door click shut, then heavy footsteps heading towards the stairs. She rolled over and strained to hear more. She heard a bedroom door slam closed then everything went silent.

The next morning, the mood in the house had been turned on its head. Her parents were surprisingly chipper and wore wide inviting smiles when Claire walked through for breakfast in her pyjamas. Her father had been cooking and she could smell sausages, bacon, and fresh coffee brewing in the kitchen. Her aunt and uncle had not yet emerged from their bedroom, but her mother was sat at the table tucking into her breakfast, wearing her dressing gown and slippers. She pulled out a chair for Claire as she entered, motioning for her to sit.

'Morning honey,' she said warmly, between bites of her toast. Her smile was convincing, but Claire wasn't fooled; her eyes betrayed the fact that she hadn't slept - heavy black bags hung beneath them and they were strained and bloodshot. *'She's barely slept an hour, at most'*, Claire can remember thinking to herself at the time. Then her father walked over carrying a large plate of freshly cooked sausages and Claire speared one with her fork and smiled up at him. His eyes were the same: red and strained. Neither of her parents had slept a wink that night.

When her aunt and uncle finally came down, they were packed and ready to leave. Adam walked behind them carrying his suitcase and looking miserable.

'Sorry we couldn't stay longer,' her uncle said, giving Claire a brief hug.

'Not a problem. We completely understand. Work comes first...' her dad replied, cheerily.

Adam walked over to Claire and hugged her sheepishly. 'See you next time, I guess.'

'Yeah, see you,' Claire replied, smiling reassuringly. But she never did see him. Years passed and the Hunt's never came to visit again. Christmases, Birthdays, Easters and New Year's Eves came and went and contact with the Hunts dwindled into nihility. Until that morning, stood outside of King's Cross Station with her umbrella shielding her and the small pile of newspapers from the beating rain, Claire hadn't seen Adam's face in over a decade.

Chapter 3
Back in the News

A full week had gone by and Claire still couldn't rid the image of her estranged cousin's face from her mind. She'd dropped her umbrella on the floor and held that picture close to her face; staring at it as the rain gradually turned it into mush.

'I can't sell that now! You'll have to buy it,' the man behind the newsstand had said to her.

Claire passed the man a pound from her purse, stashed the paper in her handbag, then made a dash for the station. Inside King's Cross, she found herself a seat next to two tussling children and read the article on the front page titled: **'Perth Man Arrested on Suspicion of Murder'.** Claire's eyes widened again as she struggled to digest what she was reading. The photo was of Adam on his wedding day with his wife Kate, who Claire had never met. She'd heard about the engagement when it happened; even vainly hoped to find an invitation through her door, though one never came. There had been no more correspondence between the Hunts' and the Beckers' since that Christmas back in ninety-seven.

Although it had been such a long time since she'd seen him, she still would have never believed her cousin capable of something like this. The way Kate had been found: the stab wounds to her neck, and in their own living room of all places! No... Adam couldn't do that... He wasn't a monster. He didn't have it in him, Claire was sure of it. But then again... time can change people; she had seen that for herself. Hadn't her own client, Asif Husain, changed to such an extent in such a short period of time that he was unrecognisable to his old teachers at his school, or even to his own parents! And not forgetting her own family and how it had changed over the years. Once a close-knit group, now frayed and unravelled. Secrets from the past left to fester, brewing mistrust and discontent between them. Like an open wound that'd become infected and left to poison the blood and connecting tissues, turning her whole family into one gangrenous green sore.

Claire had asked her mother many times about the things she had heard that night; about why her aunt and uncle never came to visit anymore; about why she hadn't seen her cousin in years. After her father had passed, her mother had closed in on herself; a shell of the person she used to be. She drank almost daily now; whether that was to deal with the pain of her father's death or to numb the guilt of a secret that was eating her from the inside, Claire could never tell. Either way, the drinking had started a long time before the accident had happened.

20

Her father, a good man in his own way, had died in a car crash not long after she'd moved to London. Claire had travelled north for the funeral and stayed with her mother and brother – who'd received compassionate leave from the army. Noah was just as tight-lipped as her mother. He rarely expressed emotion and rarely said a word to his own sister. In a way, joining the army suited his personality and he'd thrived there, quickly ascending to the rank of Lance-Corporal within a year. The fact that most of his life was spent deployed in Afghanistan was a constant worry to both her and her mother, though neither sought comfort from the other.

Sat in her kitchen in her small Camden flat, another newspaper was spread out across the table. This time the headline read: ***Prison Beating for Wife Killer***. They'd used another picture of Adam – one she'd never seen before. It was a picture of him dressed in a blue suit, being led by two police officers away from a court building. In this picture he looked a thousand years old; nearly unrecognisable from the picture taken on his wedding day in the last article. His hair had started to recede at the front and his face was creased and lined at the forehead. His eyes looked oddly dazed and distant; like the lights were on but nobody was home. He looked like a man tormented.

Claire's morning coffee had gone cold while she stared at the image for the longest time. She just couldn't reconcile the boy that she'd known with the crimes that this man had been accused of - or worse even - *with the crimes that this man had been found guilty of*. There was no killer instinct on his face, and although his eyes were dark and detached in the picture, she could still see the kindness behind them that she'd known all her life.

She picked up her coffee, took a sip, then spat the cold brew back into the cup. When she put it down, she knocked it with her arm and the drink spilled out onto the table, blotting the image of her cousin so she could no longer make out his face. She pulled the front page from the pile and scrunched it into a ball with her fists. 'Over my dead body,' she said to the empty room.

She grabbed her phone from the far end of the table and brought up its internet browser. She typed *London to Edinburgh train times* into the search engine and got a long list of trains from Kings Cross to Waverley. Although it was Sunday and she had work the next day, she booked herself on the first train in the morning. It left at 07.20am and arrived just after midday. Next, she brought up her list of contacts and placed a call to the deputy headmistress at St George's, where she worked. The woman was called Ellen and the number she was dialling was her private line. Thankfully, Claire had gotten friendly with Ellen in the months that she'd been working there. They were both single and both in their late twenties, and on more than one occasion they'd hit the bars down in Soho to share a cocktail or two while bitching about the other teachers.

After a few rings, the call connected and Ellen answered.

'Hello?'

'Ellen, it's Claire. I hope you don't mind me calling you?'

'Oh, Claire! I didn't recognise the number. Did you get a new phone? Of course not, what's wrong?'

'It's about work. I'm going to have to take a few days off. I'm having a bit of a family emergency. Long story short, I need to go up to Scotland for a few days. Is there anyway someone can cover my classes this week?'

Ellen was silent for a few seconds. Finally, she said, 'Sure. I'll call Simon, from Impact, and get them to send over another sub. Is everything ok?'

'Yeah, everything's fine. It's just something I have to deal with. Sorry for the fuss. Drinks on me when I get back?'

'Sounds good to me! Take care now. Bye!'

She hung up the phone. Claire placed her mobile back on the table and headed to the bedroom. She reached under her bed and pulled out the small travel suitcase that she hadn't used in years. She began throwing clothes in from the closet and gathering the essentials that she'd need for her trip in the morning. She went back into the kitchen and opened up her cabinet. She stood staring at the bottles. After a moment, she grabbed the bottle of Absolut vodka and stashed it in her suitcase with her toiletries.

That night Claire lay awake thinking of the journey that lay ahead. She didn't know exactly what she was planning, but she knew she wasn't going to leave her cousin to rot in a prison cell for a crime he didn't commit.

Chapter 4
Going Home

Claire had booked herself on the Virgin Express train, which had a stop at Cambridge, then straight on to Edinburgh. Arriving at King's Cross, she stopped at the newsstand again and picked up the Telegraph, hoping there wouldn't be another article about Adam in today's paper. She stuffed it in her handbag, then made her way into the station, stopping to check the departures board on her way to see if her train had started boarding – it had. She made a quick stop in WHSmith, then the toilets, then made her way to the platform.

Thirty minutes later, she was crammed into her seat with her suitcase in the overhead storage above her. She'd picked up a bottle of Diet Coke at the station, which she'd taken to the bathrooms and mixed with her vodka. She sat with her head leaned back against the headrest and sipped at the coke bottle, feeling the alcohol warm her insides. She didn't feel guilty about drinking in the morning - not anymore. At one time she had, but she'd long since accepted the drink bug ran in the family. Smoking on the other hand was something she was actively trying to quit, and she took frequent puffs on her Nicorette inhaler in between sips.

By the time the train had left Cambridge station, Claire had slipped off into an uneasy sleep with her cheek pressed against the window and her coke bottle clasped between her thighs. She woke up two hours later when the train jolted abruptly to one side. Her head bounced against the glass and her coke bottle dropped to the floor. She rubbed at her head where she'd hit it and stared out the window feeling groggy. It was snowing. Claire thought back to that Christmas spent with her family in Neilston, like she often did when it snowed. Neilston was only a ninety-minute drive from Edinburgh - if she were going to rent a car, maybe she could swing by her old neck of the woods on the way. She had no intention of visiting her mother on this trip, but something about the hillsides on the other side of the window had reminded her so strongly of her home, that she felt an almost desperate need to visit it. Then, just like that, she made up her mind; this business with Adam would have to wait. Home was beckoning. And now she'd crossed over the border into Scotland, she could no longer ignore its heralding call.

As the train pulled into Edinburgh station, she noticed the snow had sifted into rain. She quickly alighted then walked up to the Enterprise Rent-A-Car desk with her suitcase in tow and took the cheapest car they had available. She took the keys and walked up the escalators and out of the station, moving with the

crowds along Princes Street, over the bridge, around
the corner and down towards the underground car
park. She saw the Enterprise sign overhead and saw
three small Fiat 500s lined neatly against the wall near
the entrance. She clicked the unlock button on her key
and the headlights flashed on the middle one, which
was pale blue. *Perfect'*, she thought to herself, smiling.
She loaded her suitcase into the backseat and thirty
minutes later (after getting slightly lost on the busy
roads around the city centre), she was driving down
the slip road to the M8, heading west towards
Glasgow.

***

Claire saw the turnoff at the last possible second and
swerved dangerously towards it. The car that'd been
behind her issued an exasperated *beeeeep'* as it sped off
in the other direction. She realised that she might've
had one too many sips of her spiked Diet Coke on the
train. Cursing, she slapped herself hard across the face,
forcing herself to focus on the road. The sign on the
left, which she knew very well, said *'Welcome to
Neilston'*. It felt good being home, but she couldn't
bring herself to smile – not for the grim reason that
she'd come here.

Claire's old house lay on the outskirts of the town,
up a bumpy little farm road that took you to the top of
a hill that overlooked the town. She passed the old
bowling club on the right where her father had spent
many nights drinking with his buddies before
invariably getting behind the wheel and driving

himself up the farm road at closing time. *'Like father like daughter'*, she thought sourly, still tasting the bitter sting of vodka on her tongue.

The car lurched heavily as she veered left onto the bumpy road; the tiny wheels of her Fiat finding each pothole like a canyon. She turned her windscreen wipers up as the rain got heavier - she could see her old house in the distance, perched on the hill like a postcard from some American pastoral. She drove a little further then pulled up on the side, a good five-hundred metres from the house. Her mother would be home, she had little doubt of that. Her feet on the table, the cat in her lap, daytime television blaring and sipping on her third or fourth vodka of the day. She had no desire for a mother-daughter reunion on this occasion. As it so happened, she'd come here for another reason. A darker reason.

Chapter 5
Behind Closed Doors

Claire turned the key and brought silence to the engine. She sat there listening to the rain on her windscreen, wavering as to the best course of action. She knew two things for sure: first, her mother and father had been hiding something from her since she was seventeen years old – something huge. Something big enough to divide her entire family and send both of her parents into a tailspin. Second, whatever that something was had taken place, most likely, within a two-mile radius of where she sat, with the most likely places being between the house up ahead and the old off licence at the edge of town.

Her parents, as well as her aunt and uncle, had been highly intoxicated and in no fit state to drive. So, knowing her father, he would've most likely stuck to the farm roads, avoiding any unwanted attention from the law. The chances of them venturing onto the main roads and out into the town were slim – especially with her mother in the car, who had always been quite sensible. The road between the house and the off-licence was the road which she'd driven on to get here. She'd passed where the old off-licence had been at the edge of town. It had turned into a takeaway of some description (which had also closed-up shop, and some time ago by the looks of it). Admittedly, the farm road to her house had a crossroad roughly halfway along it, leading off to the old Grey farm which was long since abandoned. The Grey farm had once provided milk for the whole town. The surrounding fields were always full of cows grazing. Mr Grey, the farmer, had once allowed Claire to try her hand at milking one of his cows when she was very young. She'd liked that old man, although he'd died long before she'd reached her teens.

The fields around her now were desolate and spoiled. Void of the bountiful life which had once defined them. The possibility of a crime having been committed, and going unnoticed by the police, was slim to say the least. Though, she supposed if there had, there would've been no better place to get away it. The police force in Paisley and its suburbs had always been notoriously lax, which was probably the reason her father had handily managed to avoid a DUI for most of his life. The only time he'd been caught behind the wheel with booze in his system had unfortunately been the last drive he would ever take, drunk or otherwise. Her father had been three times the legal limit on the day two fireman had cut him from his wrecked car on the old A80 near Stepps in Glasgow. By coincidence, or by some divine twist of fate, it had been snowing on the night of the accident. Claire had been in her old flat in Marylebone when she'd received the grim news from her mother. The phone call had been short and bitter, lasting under a minute in all its magnanimous entirety. Claire flashed back on the call for the two-thousandth time.

'Hello?' Claire had laughed down the phone, having been in unusually high spirits. The phone had been quiet for all of ten seconds before the reply.

'Claire, it's your mother. I need you to listen to me,' she'd said.

'What's the matter, Mum?'

'Your father's been killed…' she said flatly.

'What…?'

'It was an accident,' she said, starting to sob and slur her words; she'd been drinking. 'There's no point coming here, it's all been arranged. Just stay where you are. The funeral is next Friday. I've already told your brother.'

When Claire went to reply, she'd already hung up. Claire dropped her phone to the floor where it smashed. Her friend, who'd just been laughing with her, hadn't understood what had happened. 'Easy there, butter fingers!' she said. Claire looked up at her and the look in her eyes made her friend recoil in fear. 'Oh my gosh! Claire! What's happened?'

She lay there curled on the kitchen floor with her friend Louise cradling her - trembling sobs breaking through her cracked lips.

***

Claire stashed the keys in her pocket and got out of the car. She could see her old house sitting silent up the road; a mist had settled over it. All the lights were off, holding darkness within, and by all outwardly appearances it was empty - though Claire knew otherwise. The house had stood for one hundred years and might stand for one hundred more. It held secrets within its walls that grew and twisted like knotweed, cracking the foundations and compromising its integrity. The house had become a metaphor for her family; a standing representation of everything they'd lived through. Claire no longer saw herself as a part of that house. She was now a lone entity; detached from its moorings, like a lifeboat cut from a sinking ship.

Claire turned abruptly - a rumbling had erupted from behind her. She watched a car, some eight-hundred feet away, turn sharply onto her road and start its tumbling climb up the hill. The black Land Rover continued past the fork, heading directly for where she was stood. She backed out of the road and stood behind her car. She held the door handle, ready to escape if she needed to.

The black car came to a stop twenty feet behind her. She watched it nervously, trying to make out the driver behind the blacked-out windscreen. The driver-side door opened, and a thin grey wellington boot protruded from the gap. She watched the man descend from the car and make his way towards her, using his arm to shield himself from the rain.

'Hello there!' he called, in a mildly Scottish accent. He walked up to the back of Claire's car and rested his hand on its hood. 'Are you lost?' He asked, curiously.

Claire struggled to see the man's face through the rain, which had suddenly gotten heavier. She peered at him under her hand. He was young – maybe around her own age. He wore a dark quilted jacket and brown corduroy trousers under his wellies, which were both splattered with mud. His face was partially shielded by a cap which was pulled low over his brow. He was tall. Much taller than Claire, who herself was quite lofty for a woman (she was the tallest in her family, apart from her father), but this man stood a good six inches taller.

'Sorry, I was just stopping for air,' Claire replied gawkily.

'Plenty of that around here,' he smiled. 'You from around here?'

'Yes, actually.' She turned back to her old house. 'I grew up here – in that house over there.'

The man stared at the house behind her and then back at Claire. 'You lived there?' he asked strangely. 'In that house?'

'Yes,' Claire replied, confused by his reaction.

'It's just… I've lived over there, my entire life.' He turned and pointed over the fields to the old Grey farm. 'Forgive me, but I don't recognise your face.'

'I'm Claire,' she stated matter-of-factly. 'Claire Becker.'

The man's brows furrowed at her words. Claire assessed him curiously, waiting for him to respond.

'I'm Kieran,' he said finally. 'Kieran Grey. I didn't know the Becker's had a daughter. How strange…'

'I didn't know the Greys had a son,' Claire replied, equally as disturbed.

'Well… I guess you never really know your neighbours,' he said, the smile returning to his face.

'I guess not…' she shrugged. '*Kieran*… is that Scottish?'

'It's Irish actually. It means *little dark one*'. I take it you're here to visit your mother then?' he asked.

'Actually… I was just leaving,' Claire replied, suddenly feeling awkward.

The man held up his hands in surrender. 'Don't let me scare you off,' he said.

'Oh, no. It's not that. I just realised that some rocks are best left unturned…'

'I see,' he replied. 'Well, on that point I couldn't agree more.'

Claire opened the car door and waved the man off as he returned to his Land Rover. She watched him in the rear-view mirror for a moment, taking a long drag on her Nicorette inhaler, then started the engine - it didn't make a sound. She turned the key again, with a little more urgency this time, but it only sputtered then failed.

'Dammit!' she scolded. She tried one last time, but again it was useless. 'Fucking Enterprise Rent-A-Car… Unbelievable.'

She looked up at the rear-view mirror and saw the Land Rover reversing. 'Shit!' She rushed out of the car and ran frantically towards it, waving her arms to get the man's attention. The Land Rover stopped, slowly reversed, then pulled up beside her and rolled down its window.

'Problem?' he asked.

'Yes. It's this damn rented car… It won't start. I'm sorry to ask you this, but do you think you could give me a lift into town? I think there's a car garage on

James Street – or at least there was twenty years ago. God knows if it's still there.'

The man paused, then said, 'I can take a look at it for you, if you like?'

'Oh, would you? That would be great. Thank you so much!'

'No problem. What are neighbours for?' He pulled his car up on the side of the dirt road and climbed out again. 'Just pop that bonnet for me, and I'll have a look under the hood.'

'Sure. Just one second.' Claire jumped back in her car and fumbled under the wheel for the lever. When her hands felt something lever-like, she gave it a little pull and heard the bonnet pop open in front of her. She watched as the tall man hooked it into place then disappeared under the hood. She could see his arms moving as he worked.

'Yep. Looks like the fuel filter is clogged. It can happen when you're too heavy on the clutch.'

Claire flushed, embarrassed.

'I can still give you a ride into town, if you like? There's no garage on James Street anymore, but there's one on Kingston Road. I know the owner; a guy named Mike. He'll have a look at it for you.'

'That would be great. Thank you so much… Kieran,' she said, remembering his name.

'No problem. Hop in.'

Claire let herself into the passenger side of the Land Rover and Kieran started the engine.

Ten minutes later, they were pulling up outside the garage on Kingston. They didn't talk much on the ride down, but thankfully it'd been a short trip. Kieran offered to stay with her as Mike, the owner of the garage, left in his truck to tow her car back into town.

Thirty minutes later, they saw his truck turn back onto the street, with Claire's rented pale blue Fiat 500, hanging from a hook at the rear.

'Looks like a clogged fuel filter,' Mike said, as he climbed out of the truck. 'Would have fixed it by the road, but I need to give it a blast with the pressurised carburetor cleaner. Gonna be about an hour or two before it's done.'

'That's fine,' Claire said, accepting that she was going to be stuck in Neilston for the time being.

'There's a pub around the corner – 'The Old House Inn', if you want to wait in there 'til it's done. They'll do you a pretty good steak pie for eight pounds. Tell them Mike sent you and they might even throw in a side of chips for free.'

Claire looked up at Kieran and shrugged. 'Fancy a pie? My treat…'

***

They found themselves a table near the back of the busy pub.

'Don't these people have work to go to?' Claire asked, taking her seat.

Kieran took off his long coat and his cap revealing his short brown hair, which was ruffled and unkempt, but suited him rather well. Under his coat he wore a navy-blue bodywarmer that revealed his thick arms and muscled physique. Claire found herself admiring it without realising, then quickly looked away.

'Bank holiday, I think,' he said, taking his own seat.

The waitress came over and took an order – two steak pies, a pint of Belhaven and a vodka Diet Coke. Not long after that, their food and drinks arrived and Claire sank her glass in two long gulps, feeling the vodka relax her chest and slow her breathing back to normal.

'Thirsty?' Kieran asked, eyeing the empty glass in her hand.

Claire laughed nervously, then began tucking into her steak pie. She realised that she hadn't eaten all day; the apprehension of visiting her old town, not to mention the repeating image of Adam's face in the newspaper, had swept all thoughts of food from her mind.

'So, what do you do?' Kieran asked, sipping at his pint.

'Lawyer,' Claire replied automatically. 'Well, at least I used to be. I'm taking a sort of a break from that life right now. I had a bit of a traumatic experience with one case that was in the news a while ago, then after that I just wanted to disappear for a while, y'know. So now I'm working as a substitute teacher. Teaching eight-year-olds in London.'

'So, that's where you shipped off to then?' he asked, slightly amused. 'What brings you back here, if you don't mind me asking?'

Claire stared back at him, wondering if she could tell this stranger the real reason she'd come home. She looked at her empty glass, wished it were full again, then guessed it didn't really matter if she did tell him

anyway. Maybe he could even help her, or he knew
something that she didn't – he had, after all, been her
neighbour (although strangely enough, she'd never
seen him before today).

'Well, the reason I came back to Neilston wasn't to
see my mother. It wasn't even to see the house. You
see, something happened to my family a long time
ago. Something secret. Something my mother and
father would never tell me, and I wanted to come back
here to the place where it happened to see if I could
work out what is was. Can you understand that? Or
am I just talking nonsense?'

'No, I can understand that,' Kieran replied
seeming interested. 'If it were my family, I'd want to
know the secret too. Can you tell me about it?'

'Not really,' Claire admitted. 'I was young – only
seventeen when it happened. It was Christmas
nineteen-ninety-seven, and really late at night. My
parents and my aunt and uncle took my dad's car into
town, I think – well the edge of town, out where the
old off-licence used to be. It was snowing really
heavily, and my brother and cousin had both gone to
bed, and I lay awake, waiting for them to get back. I
remember lying there for the longest time, wondering
why they were taking so long. I was starting to assume
the worst when, all of a sudden, I heard the car pull
back into the drive again. I heard them all get out of
the car and I heard muffled voices, like they were
arguing about something. My mother and my aunt
came into the house and went straight up to bed
without a word to one another, whereas my father and
my uncle stayed outside talking. I can't remember

what was said exactly but I know something had happened and they wanted my auntie to keep quiet about it.

'The next morning, my aunt and uncle left and then we never saw them again after that. Both my parents, who weren't exactly casual drinkers anyway, started turning to the bottle, and ever since that night it seemed that both of their lives started spinning out of control. No matter how many times I asked my mother about what happened that night, she would always say *'nothing happened'* or *'I don't know what you're talking about'*. But I know something happened. Something big. Big enough to ruin my family and drive my father to drink on the night he was killed; and I'm going to find out what it is, if it's the last thing I do...'

Kieran was glaring at her with an intensity that surprised her. 'So, does that sound pretty stupid or what?' she said, trying to lighten the mood again.

'Not stupid at all...' he replied. Claire waited for him to go on, but he didn't elaborate.

'Sooo, my plan was - well I wouldn't even call it a plan really – just drive up to Neilston and look for clues by the old house. So stupid, I know.'

'And did you find anything?'

'Nothing,' Claire replied glumly.

'Maybe you just didn't know where to look?' he suggested.

'Any suggestions?'

'I'd be willing to help. I know the area pretty well.'

Claire considered the offer briefly, then once again decided that it couldn't do any harm. She didn't even know what she was looking for, so not knowing where to look was the least of her problems.

Chapter 6
The Collector

After leaving the Old House Inn, Claire found herself
back in Kieran's Land Rover, making their way back
up the dirt road to his farm.

'I thought the place was abandoned,' she said idly,
as they turned at the fork, in the direction of the farm.

'Not abandoned, no. Well at least not to me. I
suppose to the outside world it looks like it's been
empty for years; but I'm just one person. I don't need
all that space. I just keep a single bedroom round the
back, and that suits me just fine. I don't go in the main
house very often. It's too dark and dusty and full of
old memories that don't bare remembering. Apart
from my room, the kitchen and the toilet, the rest of
the house is deserted. I considered putting it up for
sale when my folks died, but I couldn't bring myself to
part with it. Besides, I like the quiet and the privacy; it
lets me get on with my work without any
interferences.'

'And just what is it you do exactly?' Claire asked.

'I'm a collector… among other things'

'A collector? A collector of what exactly?'

He smiled. 'Nothing too strange, don't worry.'

He pulled over in the overgrown driveway at the front of the house. He led her around the side, passed an enormous barn containing rusted tractors and old bales of hay covered in black sheet plastic. The barn smelled musty and rotten; the smell of neglect and decay. Claire covered her nose to mask the stench - Kieran didn't seem to notice.

Around the back of the farmhouse was a small out-building that looked relatively newer than the rest of the house. Claire noticed that some of the windows were broken in the main house and she strained on her toes to try and see through them. Kieran coughed loudly and motioned to the back door.

'Sorry,' Claire muttered, going slightly pink. 'Just old neighbourly curiosity I guess.'

Inside the small outhouse, Claire wasn't surprised to see that the housekeeping had been neglected. Dirty plates full of old food and litter were scattered around the kitchen. Claire could see mould starting to grow on the pile that sat closest to her – she twisted her face in silent revulsion and shoved her hands in her pockets reflexively.

'I'm sorry. If I knew I was having company, I would have cleaned up a bit.' He took one of the plates and threw it into the sink, creating a deafening clatter. Claire balked but waved her hand as if it were nothing.

'Let me take you through to the sitting room,' he said quickly, seeming uncomfortable.

Claire followed as he led them through a door and down a hallway. They passed a toilet with its door hung ajar and Claire hardly dared look inside as she knew she would regret it (…she did). The sitting room was a small cupboard-like room with one couch and hardly any room for sitting. Kieran sat down and motioned for her to join him.

'Here,' he said, patting the couch beside him.

Claire stared at his hand and felt the urge to turn and bolt down the hall, back the way she'd came. *Why were they in his house again? I don't remember…* All she knew is that she'd felt extremely uncomfortable ever since stepping inside his house (if you could call it that), and she wanted to leave immediately. He smiled up at her, waiting for her to sit.

'Actually, I think I better go,' Claire said, timidly. 'I should really find somewhere to stay before it gets dark.'

Kieran raised his eyebrow, curiously. 'I haven't frightened you, have I? I just wanted to show you my collection, that was all.'

As Claire turned to leave, she could see Kieran leaning from the couch, hand outstretched towards some unseen place. As she slid one foot out the door, she heard a loud slap as he threw a large folder onto the table.

'What's that?' she asked, nervously.

'My collection,' he replied. 'I collect old newspaper clippings, as well as a bunch of other stuff.'

Claire turned and stared at the folder inquiringly, still with one hand firmly on the door handle. It was huge, like an encyclopedia-sized scrapbook with bits of old newspaper poking out from the edges. He turned the page and a small plume of dust erupted into the air.

'What year did you say it happened?' he asked, starting to flick through the pages. 'The night with your parents?'

'Nineteen-ninety-seven,' she replied, letting her grip loosen on the handle.

'It should go back that far. I've been collecting these for years. Whenever I see an interesting story, I cut it out and stick it in here. Maybe there was something in the papers from around Christmas that year? It could give us a clue as to what we're looking for.'

Claire stepped closer to the couch and rested her hand on the arm. 'You collect newspaper clippings?' she asked. 'From which papers?'

'All of them. Local papers from Neilston and Barrhead, and national ones, and some magazines too, if I see something I like. Oh, here we are, ninety-seven. I have some clippings from that year.'

Claire sat on the couch next to him, disregarding her urgent will to leave. She looked at the pages that he'd opened the book out to; there were dozens of clippings all pasted shabbily to the page. She began combing through them, reading the headline of each; searching for something – anything – that could help.

'What about this one?' he asked, pointing to a small yellowing clip that was hidden under two larger ones. The title read simply: *'Neilston Woman Feared Missing'*. Kieran pulled out the clip and lay it flat on top of the others. It was only a small article, merely a paragraph.

Susan Laing (58, of Broadlie Road, Neilston) who was reported missing on Boxing Day, hasn't been seen by family or friends in nearly a week. Her son, Thomas Laing (21), who lives alone with his mother in their three-bedroom home on Broadlie Road, has told police in Barrhead that he hasn't seen or heard from his mother in nearly a week. The young man first raised the alarm on December 26th, when Ms Laing didn't return home after visiting a friend. Police are currently investigating the disappearance. More to follow…

Claire re-read the clipping for the third time, then fell back on the couch.

'You don't suppose your parents had something to do with that?' he asked. 'Seems like an awful coincidence that a woman would be reported missing on the day your parents would disappear in the car for three hours – and then act so strangely afterwards?'

Claire knew he was right, but she didn't want to believe it. She leaned forward to stare at the scrapbook again, desperately searching for more on the story of Ms Laing.

'There!' she gasped, pointing at the page. She'd spotted another article on the same yellowing paper as the first.

Neilston Woman Found Alive and Well:
Susan Laing (58, of Broadlie Road, Neilston) who was reported missing on 26th December last year, has since been found alive and well in the Govan area of

Glasgow. It seems Ms Laing had been living with an elderly man in a flat she'd once owned in the seventies. Although it was previously unknown, Ms Laing has since been diagnosed with early onset-dementia and is receiving treatment at her home with her son Thomas, 21.

Claire felt a wave of relief wash over her as she read the article. She knew she'd been silly for even entertaining the notion that her parents could've be involved in something as heinous as what she'd momentarily been thinking. Kieran had read the article with her but didn't seem as pleased. He had spotted something else on the page and had begun unsticking it from the book. He lay the new article on the table.

Car Found Abandoned:
An abandoned car was reported to police on Monday morning, having been found in woodland area near Barrhead, East Renfrewshire. The car, showing signs of an impact to the rear, had traces of blood on the dashboard and the steering wheel, though no body has been found as of yet. Police are currently looking to question anyone who may have knowledge of the car or its owner. Strangely, the licence plates on the vehicle have been removed and no documentation was left inside, leaving police with difficulty in tracing its registered owner.

The date on the article said January 1st, 1998. Claire knew Barrhead was only one town over from Neilston and a mere fifteen-minute drive away.

'Is there anything else on that story?' she asked Kieran, tracing through the page with her finger.

'I'm looking,' he replied. He flicked over the page and began tracing through the articles there.

'Anything?' She asked again.

'It doesn't look like it...'

Claire pulled her phone from her coat pocket, flipped it open then typed in the passcode to unlock it and brought up the browser. She typed *'abandoned car missing driver Barrhead'* into Google and began skimming through the search results on the Nokia N95's screen. Kieran edged closer and peered over her shoulder as she scrolled down the page.

On the second page of results, Claire came across the article that they'd just read on the clipping. The web page opened into an old archive of BarrheadNews articles. She selected the heading and a new window opened with an image of the abandoned car in question. Like the images from her memory of that winter, the ground was covered in snow. The car, which was blue and damaged at the back, clearly had the licence plates ripped from its bumpers. It appeared to have been involved in some sort of collision and from the look of the snow and debris from the trees on the windshield, had been sitting there for at least a few days, maybe more.

'Do you know where that picture is taken?' she asked, peering at the screen. Kieran shook his head and said he didn't. This area of Renfrewshire was overrun by woodland and forests. In fact, last year, Reader's Digest had voted East Renfrewshire as the second-best place in the United Kingdom to raise a family. The magazine had even visited and cited Barrhead in their decision. Claire had found this article quite amusing when she'd come across it some months back while reading an old copy of the magazine in her doctor's surgery waiting room.

The fact Barrhead and its surrounding neighbourhoods were so greatly sought after was in large part due to their remoteness and the wildness of the woodlands in the area. A mere thirty minutes from the hustle and bustle of busy Glasgow, was this scenic Scottish hamlet, set amongst the Scottish countryside with the cream of the country's flora and fauna at your doorstep. While this was all well and good for house prices in the area, it proved a challenge when trying to navigate yourself, as everywhere looked the same, making it the perfect place to get away with a crime such as, for instance, a hit and run.

Claire scrolled through the rest of the results on her phone but could see nothing linking back to the abandoned car from the previous article.

'It could be nothing?' Kieran offered.

Or everything… Claire thought.

Chapter 7

Bones

As Kieran closed the scrapbook and stashed it back in his cabinet, Claire let out a long-tired sigh of frustration. It had been a very long day and they were working with scraps here. What they had found was nothing to go on. Some lady with dementia who'd gotten lost then turned up in a flat owned by a pensioner in Govan a week later, and some abandoned car with its licence plates stolen and blood on the steering wheel but no body in the driver seat. Both had, coincidently, happened around New Year ninety-eight, one week after the supposed incident that had left her parents so utterly and hopelessly changed; but whether these incidents that had made the local news had anything to do with her family she could not tell. Did one of these events lead to the collective downfall of her parents and the subsequent collapse of their marriage, shortly followed by the death of her father, then some years later, the death of her aunt as well? Was her father now lying beneath a headstone in

Neilston cemetery due to some guilt that he felt for an incident that happened that Christmas?

Speaking of her father's tombstone, it had been a long time since she'd visited it. Ok, that was a lie – she'd never visited it. In fact, she'd never seen her father's headstone. She'd been there on the day of his funeral but there'd been no headstone above his plot on that occasion. Her mother had made all the arrangements and organised the headstone with its inscription that read simply *Beloved husband and father, taken too soon'*.

Although her parents were never officially divorced, they had however been separated for over a year at the time of her father's passing - a fact her mother had chosen to overlook while selecting an inscription.

'What are you thinking?' Kieran asked, looking up at her.

'I'm thinking… that I'd like to visit my father's grave,' she said with some hesitation. Perhaps the time had come to set aside their old differences and reacquaint herself with her father.

***

Neilston graveyard lay at the other side of town, on the hillside opposite the one on which the initial occupants of her parent's house had first plotted their home. As far as graveyards go, especially for one in Scotland, it was decidedly creepy. A large gothic archway at the entrance led into a necropolitan jungle of imposing winged angels and elaborately crafted crypts that housed entire families going back all the way to the late seventeen-hundreds and thereafter. It was a place Claire had been terrified of as a little girl and a place she would never dream of entering alone, especially not at this time of day - the gradually darkening sky above them, slowly drifting into night.

Kieran had grabbed a torch from the backseat of his car, in which he'd offered to once again drive her, seeing as Claire's own car was still waiting for her at the garage. She didn't know why Kieran was doing all this to help her, but she suspected his motives lay beyond those of mere neighbourly consideration. Regardless, she needed him right now – in fact, she needed all the help she could get, to get to the bottom of the mystery surrounding that night that now plagued her.

Claire led the way through the archway at the entrance. Away from the streetlamps and headlights of the outside world, darkness had fallen around them. Claire found it odd that she could be as grownup as she chose to be, when she was in a courtroom or liaising with a barrister or getting fucked from behind over her desk by a paralegal, yet when she stepped inside a graveyard, she felt instantly like a child again; where things such as ghosts and vampires and all those things that graced the pages of horror stories and were nonentities in the grownup world, were once again possible and unknown.

Kieran rolled the flashlight over the dark rows of stones, illuminating each one briefly like a slideshow of tarot cards. The high priestess, the fool, the magician, the lovers, the hermit, the empress and death

– all standing like some unworldly battalion, ready to charge at them.

'Which way?' Kieran asked, as they approached the first fork in the path.

Claire thought back to the day of her father's funeral. On that day she had walked without knowing where her feet were taking her. It was entirely a blur of mixed tears filled with both sadness and resentment. She'd followed the procession with her mother and her brother, not taking note of which way they were walking, or for how long they walked. Those details were as inconsequential as what she'd eaten for breakfast that morning – or at least they had been at the time.

'Maybe left?' Claire replied, not feeling very sure, but also starting to not really care at the same time. There had been a reason she hadn't come back here in so long, and it wasn't that she was cruel or uncaring or that she didn't want to see her father again. The reason was that she had locked all these feelings in a box in order to carry on with her life in the only way she knew how – to knuckle down with her studying and throw herself into her work. When your mind is kept full of things like 'slugs in a bottle of ginger beer' (Donoghue vs Stevenson, 1932) or 'can a man be guilty of raping his wife?' (R vs R, 1991), it doesn't leave much room for things like grieving for lost parents.

As they swerved left down the path, and Kieran's flashlight swung with them, Claire pushed her mind to remember anything she could from that day at the funeral. She could picture the plot on which her father had been buried. There were flowers, lots of flowers, and lots of people dressed in black. Claire could see herself standing amongst them, watching as the pallbearers lowered her father slowly into his grave. She had looked to her left and seen her brother standing next to her – shorter in height, yet stocky and strong, and wearing a rented black suit that was two sizes too small for him. She had looked to her right and seen her mother holding the arm of her sister (Claire's aunt Deborah) and flanked by her two brawny sons (Claire's cousins, Michael and Robert).

Behind them had been a very peculiar statue (or headstone rather). It was as unnerving a headstone as she could ever remember laying eyes on, but at the time it had been blurred into the background, along with everything else that was there. The headstone was a statue of a ghostly white woman leaning precariously forward to the extent that she seemed to be defying gravity. The effect was such that to the casual observer it appeared that she was floating above her grave – attached to it only by the tiniest thread of unseen marble at her feet. The illusion of it floating was not what made this headstone so creepy, however; it was the expression on her face. Not one of peaceful serenity, like you would expect, but one of anguish and terror. The more she pushed into the recesses of her memory, the clearer the face became in Claire's mind.

'We're looking for a headstone,' she said suddenly, breaking the silence.

'Well, that should be easy,' Kieran replied. 'We're surrounded by them.'

'A white headstone,' she corrected. 'Of a woman. A woman who looks like she's in pain…'

Kieran's eyebrows furrowed as he dissected what she'd told him. He shrugged and started combing through the rows of stones in front of them with his flashlight. They followed the path around as it wound them deeper into the darkness, away from the last remaining glow of the streetlamps behind them. Claire shivered as her eyes adjusted to the blackness. Each moment they spent in this graveyard was bringing back more unwanted memories from the funeral. She had been perfectly happy keeping these things locked away in the annals of her mind. They had been recorded and logged, then chronologically filed under *'Do not Open!'*, along with those other things from her childhood that she couldn't bare remembering. That was of course until she'd come back to her hometown and forced open Pandora's Box to see what was inside; simultaneously checking-out every restricted book in her own personal library of recollections. Not that it mattered now, the damage had been done.

'Over there!' Kieran shouted abruptly, using his flashlight to illuminate the headstones to his left. Claire turned and her eyes brushed over the stones that were nearest to them. There was an enormous mausoleum with large flying buttresses, reminiscent of those adorning Notre-Dame in Paris. Behind the mausoleum, Claire saw what he was pointing at – it was the floating woman in white, hovered between the headstones. Her marble face a frozen picture of torment.

***

They walked across the grass, weaving through the graves and ornately crafted headstones, arriving at the statue of the woman in white.

'Jesus,' Kieran said, noticing her face. 'What happened to her?'

Claire didn't answer. She was searching the headstones around them for any sign of her father. Then she saw him, and at the same moment a flashback hit her so hard that she almost stumbled on her heels. She was back at the funeral and she was standing beside her brother. Noah was looking emotionlessly on as their father was lifted, then slowly lowered with purple laced rope into the long, eight-foot-deep hole that was dug in front of them. Her mother had begun howling and her mother's sister had hurried over to comfort her. In a moment of distraction, that would likely haunt the young man responsible, as well as everyone else that was there that day, for the rest of their lives, one of the pallbearers lost his hold and the rope slipped through his hands, causing the coffin to lurch dangerously to one side. As the man tried frantically to reach out and grab the remaining rope before it slipped down the hole, the pallbearer beside him was shoved out of the way, causing his own rope to slip uselessly through his fingers. Unable to bear the load of the coffin alone, the remaining four men faltered. They frantically worked to correct the situation, but it was too late… The coffin lid unclasped, and the coffin flew open, revealing her father's ashen corpse hung precariously to one side in an upright seated position. For a moment, Claire thought that he would float like the statue of the woman in white that hovered nearby, but it only lasted for an instant. Her father toppled forward as the weight of gravity took over. He fell sideways from the coffin, dropping clumsily from the plush satin interior into the open grave below.

Screams and cries erupted from the onlookers as men and women rushed forward to help the last remaining pallbearers as they clung desperately to the rope to stop the coffin from falling, but it was no use; the weight of the heavy American-style casket was too much for them to bear. The coffin dropped heavily, making an almighty clatter as it tumbled into the hole on top of her father.

Claire gasped as the traumatic incident played before her eyes. How could she have forgotten? What had happened that day had been so unbearably awful that she'd buried it under mountains of grey matter in the furthest possible corners of her mind; disconnecting all synapses and points of neuropathic contact so she couldn't possibly think about it, no matter how hard she tried. These walls had of course been toppled as soon as she'd walked into the cemetery. The most painful memory of her life was now on repeat in her head; she squeezed her eyes in frustration, desperately trying to erase it again.

'You ok?' Kieran asked hesitantly. 'You're starting to look a bit like this white headstone over here.'

'I'm fine,' Claire lied. 'I just remembered something that happened here.'

She walked over to her father's headstone, trying with all her waking might to block all the awful memories that were streaming back to her in droves.

Kneeling at the grave, her hand shot to her mouth and she screamed. Thrown into action by the sound, Kieran came sprinting up behind her and threw himself to the ground by her side. He placed one hand on her shoulder and together they stared at the headstone. Written diagonally across the middle, in chaotic red spray-paint, was the word *'Killer'*…

Chapter 8
Haunted

Claire felt the dampness soak through her jeans. She'd been kneeling on the wet grass for over a minute; unable to move or look away from the headstone. The paint was fresh; sprayed within the last week by the looks of it. Kieran turned to look at her, gauging her expression as she stared dead ahead.

'Perhaps... it's time to visit your mother after all?' he said, carefully.

Claire raised her hand and touched the paint where it coloured her father's middle initial. She traced her finger along the groove of the letter and tried to remember the last time she had spoken the name out loud. She whispered it under her breath and the word tasted strange on her tongue; the way her own name sometimes did when she repeated it over and over until the word lost all meaning. She felt guilty saying the name, even to herself. Had she been a bad daughter? Had she been neglectful of her mother? And of her father, while he'd been alive?

The prospect of visiting her mother terrified her even more than the memory of her father's funeral. She had become a distant woman since the death of her husband. The mother Claire had once cuddled up to on the couch in the evenings was now well and truly gone. The person that was left was unrecognisable from the kind and gentle protector she remembered as a child. Their last meeting had been another memory confined to the deepest reaches of her subconscious - a memory that she was only recalling now due to absolute necessity, for otherwise the thought of it would be unbearable.

It had been Christmas (again) on the year of her father's passing. Claire, on invitation, had made her way back to Scotland, after a tough year studying for her exams, to spend the holidays with her mother and brother – what was left of their family. Noah's first deployment in Afghanistan had instilled in him a quiet circumspection, like he'd looked death in the face and had lived to tell the tale and was now wary of anything that might damage his newfound perception of reality.

Claire's life had been turned upside down again that year after an incident that occurred while returning home from a night out that she'd spent with some friends from university. Claire had left the group early, giving the excuse that she had a tonne of revision to do in morning (owing to her upcoming torts exam that she was criminally underprepared for). She walked out of the bar, where they'd spent most of the evening, with the intention of getting a taxi back to her flat in Marylebone. When she'd seen the size of the queue at the taxi rank, she'd been forced to consider other options.

The tube had been a possibility, of course, from Covent Garden station, but any sensible lady (like Claire had considered herself to be at the time), would be fully aware of the history of petty crime that occurred on the London Underground after dark and would use it only as a last resort and nothing more.

She decided to walk to see if she could flag down a taxi. She walked alone through Leicester Square then along Charing Cross Road, taking a shortcut through Soho Square, past the old gardener's hut and the statue of Charles II, then exited onto Carlisle Street.

On Carlisle Street, outside the Toucan Bar, there was a man leaning against a blue door, smoking a cigarette. The bar beside him was just closing up and Claire assumed he must have worked there. He whistled as Claire passed her, but she ignored him and walked quicker. Catcalls, wolf whistles and lurid chants were a sad part of life for young women living in big cities, and it was hardly the first time Claire had experienced it.

She passed the Nadler hotel, with its statue of a fairy that seemed to watch her as she walked. She checked her watch and saw it was approaching 2am. The street was unusually quiet for that time of night, though she supposed it was approaching winter and a lot of people didn't want to brave the cold. She turned onto the alley beside the hotel and heard movement behind her. She glanced over her shoulder and saw the man from the Toucan Bar had followed her. He was a young man, wearing a trendy jacket and had neatly styled hair. He looked like the type that would've worked in a bar or a clothes shop or a restaurant. Maybe she'd dropped something without realising and he was returning it to her? She checked her purse and then her pockets, but everything was accounted for. What did he want then?

'Not going to say hello? That's very rude,' he said, catching up to her.

Claire didn't stop and kept her head facing forward. 'Do I know you?' she asked.

'I'm Simon. Everybody knows me,' he joked.

Claire turned to face him and noticed he was quite handsome. He looked to be in his early twenties. He had blonde hair and short well-groomed stubble on his cheeks. 'I'm sorry, I don't know you,' she said, turning away again.

'Well, you can get to know me,' he urged confidently. 'I'm a nice guy, I promise.'

'No thanks,' Claire replied, with what she thought was an air of finality.

'Why are you being rude?' he asked, feigning dejection.

Claire ignored him. This guy was chancing his luck and she wanted to get away from him as quickly as possible.

'Let me walk you home?' he offered. 'I wouldn't mind seeing where you live…'

Claire rolled her eyes and quickened the pace. The man had to jog just to keep up with her now. The street they'd turned onto was dark and deserted. She was starting to feel scared; this guy just didn't seem to be taking the hint.

'What's your name?' he asked, walking beside her now.

Claire didn't answer.

'Hey! I said what's your name?' He grabbed the strap on her handbag and Claire swung around, clinging onto the other end.

'Let go!' she screamed at him.

'What's your problem?' he yelled back. 'I just want to know your name!'

'Why won't you fuck off?' she shrieked. The man yanked the handbag from her grip with one violent tug. Claire ran at him, desperately grabbing for the bag which the man held out of her reach. She stood on her tiptoes trying to grab at the strap, but it was too high for her.

'You're fucking crazy, you know that?' The man laughed, as they grappled.

Claire heard laughing close by. A group of young people had turned onto the street. They stopped when they saw the commotion, then turned away quickly, not wanting to get involved.

'Help!' Claire screamed after them, but it was no use – they were already gone. The man looked down at her and shrugged.

'You want the bag back?' he asked.

Claire nodded eagerly.

'Well… you're going to have to do something for me,' he said.

Claire used her heal to skewer the man's foot. He bent down in agony and Claire grabbed the handle of her bag. The man pulled the other side with an almighty tug and Claire went crashing to the ground, taking the man with her. He rolled on top of her and pinned both her wrists with his hands.

'Now see what you've done,' he said, laughing as Claire started to cry. She'd tripped and broken the heel of her shoe as they'd fallen, and her ankle had twisted beneath her - she tried desperately to ignore the pain as she felt it starting to swell.

'All you had to do was tell me your fucking name. Now look what you've done…'

Claire hid her face to the side and searched the street for any sign of more passers-by. She couldn't believe this was happening to her. 'Please stop,' she choked, as the tears streamed down her face.

The man reached behind him and felt the cool of her thigh beneath her skirt. She squirmed desperately to get away, but the man's weight held her down. She could feel his hand sliding up her leg and she thought she might be sick if he went any further. His hand reached the warm material of her panties and she kicked out her legs in terror, screaming at him to *'STOP!'*

He stared down at her and told her to shut her fucking mouth. As his reaching fingers moved to pull her panties to the side, Claire heard shouting from somewhere close by.

'Oi! What the fuck are you doing?' Someone yelled, and Claire heard his slapping footsteps against pavement. 'Get the fuck off of her!'

The stranger was almost upon them when her attacker retracted his hand from between her legs and scrambled to the side. He scurried to his feet and bolted down the street and around the corner, just as the stranger arrived at her side.

'Are you ok?' he asked urgently, getting down on his knee and placing his hand on her shoulder.

Claire squirmed violently at the touch and screamed into the night.

'It's ok,' said the stranger. 'He's gone now. I'm going to phone the police.'

***

Claire's ordeal had happened five weeks before Christmas. She couldn't bring herself to tell her friends about what had happened to her until many months later. She felt ashamed and embarrassed; like she was to blame for what the man had done to her. It was her fault for wearing that short skirt and low-cut top that night, and it was her fault for not waiting for a taxi like she'd planned to. It was also her fault for wanting to leave early and study and it was her fault for going out in the first place when she had an exam on Monday morning.

The torts exam, unsurprisingly, had been a complete and utter disaster, after failing to get any sleep since the incident. The police had been in contact with her the next morning and she'd spent Saturday afternoon in Charing Cross Police Station, going over the details of her attacker with a sketch artist.

Simon Matthew Feldon was caught two weeks later in his flat in West Brompton - little rich boy had been living off his parent's bloated bank account for most of his life and wasn't used to being told 'no'. He was jailed for two years in the spring. He'd be out by the time he was twenty-six and would be able to prowl the streets of London again, looking for his next victim. By the time of the trial, she had told her friends about what had happened, and Claire's friend Louise had gone with her and sat in the gallery while she took the stand and testified against him.

The man who'd come to her rescue was called Bobby Lindley – he'd just finished his shift at the Nadler Hotel and was on his way home when he saw the commotion down the street. Claire had never thanked the man personally – she'd never been able to find the courage to contact him for fear he'd want to talk about what he'd seen that night. He'd been at the trial and Claire had managed a smile at him... but that was the most she was up to - anymore was pushing it.

By the time Christmas arrived that year, the last thing Claire felt like doing was visiting her family. She'd spent most of the month of December in bed, avoiding the calls and text messages that her friends left her and missing a whole month's worth of university, that would take her ages to catch up on. She hadn't told her mother about what had happened to her (she hadn't told anybody yet, apart from the police).

She hadn't seen her mother since the funeral, so she didn't know what to expect. The sole text message she'd received from her, inviting her to come home, had been both short and bitter, in true mother style. She'd watched her mother spiral slowly out of control over the years, and she suspected, now that her father had died, that matters had gotten a whole hell of a lot worse.

***

Somehow, through sheer grit and determination, she had managed to drag herself out of bed that day, pack herself a small suitcase and make her way to the train station. She'd taken the Virgin Express train, which had a stop at Cambridge, then straight on to Edinburgh. From there, she would catch a cab which would take her the ninety-minute drive west, across Scotland, to Neilston, and likely cost her in the region of one-hundred pounds. When she arrived at her house in Neilston, she would greet her mother and her brother, stick around for an hour or two and have a polite drink and exchange small talk, then she would get back in her bed and stay there. That was the plan.

When the taxi finally pulled up at the end of her road (the driver had refused to take his car up it due to the crater-sized potholes) it had cost her eighty-nine-fifty, so she'd nearly been right. She paid the man with the five twenties she had anyway, which included his tip (something she always gave grudgingly, if at all, but today she felt generous – either that or she simply didn't care anymore).

There was no welcome party at the door, but she knew better than to expect one. She let herself in using the key under the plant pot. Inside, the lights were turned off, which was strange. It felt cold and unwelcoming. There were no Christmas decorations hanging from the staircase, like there had once been on

Christmases of old. She could see the fireplace was roaring in the backroom – the light from it flickered against the walls in the hall and she could hear the crackling of its flames. She pushed open the door and saw her mother in an armchair in front of the fire - she was wrapped in a blanket. Noah was stood in the corner by the window, watching the rain twist and curve as it ran in thin estuaries down the glass.

'Hello mother,' Claire said, closing the door gently behind her.

She seemed to startle at her voice as if breaking from a daydream.

'Oh, Claire! You're home!' she gasped, looking up in bewilderment. 'I'm so happy you could make it. Noah dear, fix your sister a drink, won't you?'

Noah pushed himself from the window with his shoulder - his hands still inside his pockets - and walked towards his sister.

'Good to see you,' he said, although he didn't seem to mean it. He looked rather dazed as well - as if her intrusion had roused them both from some deep slumber.

'Vodka Diet Coke?' he asked, moving to the minibar and lifting the bottle of Absolut that was nearly empty.

'Yes please,' she replied, taking a seat on the long couch behind her.

'How've you been?' Noah asked, dropping two cubes of ice into a glass.

'Ok. And you?'

'Ok. It's been a while…'

'Yeah, since the funeral I think.' She cringed as soon as the words had left her mouth. She hadn't meant to say it, but she hadn't been thinking; the journey had been long, and she was tired. She turned to her mother. 'I'm sorry. I didn't mean to…'

Her mother still stared into the fireplace. The flickering light sent shadows dancing off the walls around her. Noah arrived at her side, holding out a glass. She took it and immediately took a drink. The vodka was strong and warming. She took another, then set it down on the table in front of her.

'Come on. I'll help you with your bag,' he said.

Noah led Claire out into the hallway and shut the door behind them, sealing their mother in the backroom alone. He picked up her suitcase and she followed him through to the bedroom.

Her old room was exactly the way she'd left it. It looked kind of old-fashioned for a young woman's bedroom, but she liked it all the same. Her favourite part of the room was the large antique bed that took up the majority of the floor-space. The wooden headboard was made from solid mahogany and had ornate floral hand-carvings adorning its bone china blue colour palette. Claire had always treasured this bed as the one thing in the house that had been truly her own. When she'd moved down to London to attend university, she'd asked her parents if she could take the bed with her, but they'd refused, telling her that the bed would be here waiting for her whenever she came home.

'I'll let you get unpacked,' Noah said, closing the door behind him.

Alone now, Claire threw her suitcase on the bed and kicked off her shoes. She lay there for a moment with her eyes closed, feeling herself sink into her old duvet, which was so much softer than the one she had in London.

***

She awoke with a start, sometime later. It was dark outside now. Her curtains were still open, and the moonlight flooded the room, illuminating her dresser and her wardrobe and her old -

'Shit!' Her hands flew to her side and she sat bolt upright in the bed - there was someone sitting in the corner of her room.

'Hello dear,' her mother said serenely.

'Oh mother, it's you! You gave me such a fright…'

'I didn't want to wake you - you looked so peaceful lying there.'

'Is there something I can help you with?' Claire asked, confused as to why she was here.

'You didn't say goodnight. I just wanted to check on you. Can a mother not check on her daughter anymore?'

'Of course. I just thought something might be wrong.'

'Nothing's wrong dear. You always loved that bed so much; it was nice to see you sleeping in it again. It belonged to your grandmother; did you know? She loved that bed too. When she got sick, she didn't leave that bed for months. In fact, she died in that bed, did you know?'

Claire cringed. 'Someone died in this bed?'

'Yes dear,' her mother smiled. 'Your grandmother. Anyway, I'll be getting on. Goodnight dear.' She closed the door behind her, leaving Claire sitting in her bed, where she remained, sleepless until morning.

Chapter 9
Hereditary

Claire never slept in her favourite bed again. It was approaching nine o'clock now and Kieran was driving them up the bumpy farm road towards the house - the memories from the last time she'd visited, ripe, at the forefront of her mind. He pulled up the car in the pebbled driveway and turned to face Claire.

'Are you sure you want to do this?' he asked.

Claire wasn't sure at all. She had had no intention of visiting her mother when she'd arrived back in Neilston; but too many questions needed answering. The spray-paint on her father's headstone had been the deciding factor. Surely, she would know about it.

'Do you want me to wait in the car?' he asked, idling the engine.

Claire was about to say, *'that would probably be for the best'*, but she stopped herself, changing her mind. 'Actually, would you mind coming in with me?' she asked.

She didn't know why but for some reason she felt safer with this man around; and she definitely wasn't up to facing her mother again alone.

'If you're sure? he asked. 'I wouldn't want to intrude.'

'No intrusion at all. You're her neighbour, remember?'

Kieran smiled and they both stepped out of the car. Claire stood for a second facing the house; how could somewhere she'd once loved so much, now seem so frightening to her? It seemed unfathomable that she had once played in that garden and she'd learned to ride a bike on this very driveway where she was standing. As she stood there, hushed and still, she could have sworn that the house was not a monster after all, but lived and breathed as it had lived before. She tried to ignore the fact that the grass had grown wild and overrun and the windows had turned opaque with the layers of dust and grime. There were no lights on in the house, and for all anybody would know just by looking at it, it was empty.

Claire led them to the door and picked out the key from underneath the plant pot. She let out a long slow breath as she inserted it into the keyhole – what was she getting herself into?

The house felt cold and was dark, like the last time she'd been there. 'Hello?' she called out. 'Mother? It's me, Claire. Are you there?'

There was no answer. Kieran followed her inside and she closed the door behind them. She wouldn't have thought it possible, but the place had grown wilder in the years since she'd been there. There was dirt and leaves on the floor – foliage left to fester - and the air was thick with dust and the smell of rot. The house had taken on a habitat of its own. It felt arrogant and hating, a house without kindness. *This house is vile*, she realised. *It's vile, it's diseased; get away from here at once!*

Claire expected her mother would be in the backroom, under a blanket by the fire, but when she creaked open the door, she saw the room was empty. The fire hadn't been lit in a long time from the looks of it. Charred kindling and coals had fallen onto the tiles and the poker lay strewn across the carpet. There was a half empty bottle of Smirnoff beside the couch, and a fallen glass along with it that lay on its side.

Claire looked anxiously toward Kieran, who was peering up the staircase. she felt relieved that she'd invited him to come along with her, as she was positive that she wouldn't have the nerve to ascend those stairs alone.

Kieran nodded up the stairs as she arrived by his side. 'After you,' he said, gesturing with his hand.

Claire gulped and placed her foot on the first creaky step, which sent a crunching noise echoing around the hall. She placed her hand on the banister and took the steps slowly, feeling her foot sink into the wood with each step and the accompanying creak that went with it.

'Are you sure someone's home?' Kieran whispered, from behind her.

She shrugged. 'I don't know...'

On the landing that separated the ground floor from the first, Claire caught a glimpse of the guest bedroom, that had its door hanging open. There were no lights on, but she could hear a faint swishing sound coming from within. She stood motionless; the noise growing in her ears like the swarming of bees. She pointed to the open door and Kieran nodded.

She took the last few steps as carefully as she could, balancing her weight on her heels to avoid the loud creaking. She was sure that if anyone were upstairs, they would by now have been alerted to their presence. As they approached the door, the buzzing sound got louder and she could see the door moving, ever so slightly, as the sound grew. She placed her fingers around the door handle and opened it gently, anticipating the onslaught from whatever dwelt within.

'Mother, are you there? It's me, Claire?'

As she stepped inside the room, she was hit by a powerful gust of wind. Her hair whipped out behind her and she was thrown against the wall, blinded by the force of the gale blowing into her.

'Fuck!' She shrieked, as Kieran rushed into the room after her. He ran towards the window, shielding his eyes with one hand, and slammed the heavy wooden shutters closed. There was silence.

'Fuck…' she said again, catching her breath. 'How long has that been open?'

'I'm not sure,' Kieran replied. 'But it certainly explains all the leaves.'

'It's freezing.' She shivered then wrapped her cardigan across her chest, hunching her shoulders against the chill.

'I think the house is empty.'

Claire looked at him, knowing he was right. 'Where is she?' she asked, not expecting a reply.

Claire hurried to check the rest of the upstairs before leaving. She pushed open the toilet door and closed it again quickly. The smell was revolting - the bathtub had turned green with mildew. She heard Kieran slowly creak open the door to the master bedroom and she rushed across the landing to follow him. As soon as he turned the handle, the smell from inside started creeping out through the crack, like he'd just opened the lid on some ungodly jar of excrement.

'Wait! I'll do it...'

Kieran dropped his hand to his side and Claire stepped in front of him, pushing the door forward and balking as the power of the smell engulfed her. The smell was like nothing she'd ever encountered; too horrible to put legibly into words. Like rotting meat, mixed with shit and mould. The way an open wound might smell if it turned gangrenous and was set upon by maggots.

Inside the bedroom, a single beam of light from the window streamed through the open curtains and onto the bed. On the bed, the sheets were pulled back revealing the mattress underneath. Her mother lay face down in a pool of dried blood on the mattress.

Claire screamed and backed into Kieran, who'd stepped into the bedroom behind her. She turned and buried her face in his chest. Written on the wall behind the bed, in chaotic red spray-paint, just the way it'd been on the headstone, was the word *Killer*.

Chapter 10
Almanac

Claire awoke in a room she had no memory of entering. The lamp next to her bed had fallen to the floor and her jeans and the rest of her clothes had been hastily bundled into the chair in the corner. She noticed the *Do Not Disturb* sign on the door and it all came flooding back to her. After the dreadful moment they'd found her mother's body in her bedroom, Kieran had quickly telephoned the authorities. Claire had been hysterical and was consoled for most of the evening in the back of a police car by a very understanding officer who happened to be one of her old friends from school.

Once the house had been sealed off and the crime scene team had moved in, they'd been taken away in a police car to the station. They gave a statement to an officer called, Constable Morgan, who'd arranged for a taxi to take Claire to the nearest hotel, once she was satisfied that she had everything she needed for now. She'd told Claire that she'd likely be wanted for further questioning in the days to come and to stay in the area for the time being.

Claire had said goodbye to Kieran at the station and promised to call him in the morning, once she'd gotten herself together. The hotel was called Dalmeny Park and was a five-minute drive away, in Barrhead. After checking in and taking the stairs to the third floor, Claire had raided the minibar. Four empty bottles of travel-sized Absolute vodka lay beside the bed. Her suitcase, still in her car, which she was yet to pick up, contained the full-sized equivalent and would have saved her the added expense of the overpriced amenities (the fact she was thinking about money right now was testament to how little sentiment she had left for her mother).

Throwing back the cover, she dragged herself from the bed. She walked over to the en-suite bathroom and looked at herself in the mirror. Her hair was crimped into spectacular hedge animals. She ran the tap and splashed her face with some water, feeling some of the hangover start to diminish. In her handbag she found a comb and some painkillers. She took three ibuprofen then ran the comb through her hair. She'd slept with her contacts in again, which explained why her vision was distorted. She dried her hand on a towel, then, using a finger, flicked the dried disks from her eyes into the sink.

She rummaged in the bag for her glasses and found them beneath her compact. Next, she searched for her phone, finding it in the pocket of her coat. Displayed on the screen was a text message alert.

Phone me when you wake up. Kieran

Claire selected the 'call back' option on her screen and the phone started dialling.

'Hello?'

'Kieran, it's me, Claire. I got your text… Where did you get my number?'

'Claire, good. I got it from Mike at the garage. Anyway, listen… I think I've found something… Can you meet me?'

'Sure. Where?'

'Meet me at the Old House Inn. One hour?'

'Sure.' Claire hung up the phone. She knew now more than ever that she needed to find out what happened to her family. She threw her mobile on the bed and instead picked up the receiver on the landline. She hit '9' and waited for it to dial.

'Reception,' said a cheery voice from downstairs.

'Hi. My name's Claire Becker, in room 307. I need you to call me a taxi.'

'Of course, Miss Becker. I'll phone one for you now. It should be around fifteen minutes?'

'That's fine. Thank you.' Claire hung up the receiver.

Fifteen minutes later, she was showered and dressed and waiting for her taxi in the lobby.

'Miss Becker?'

Claire looked up. The girl behind the reception desk was looking at her.

'Miss Becker, I have a phone call for you. It's a Mike Brittle?'

Claire stood up and walked towards reception. 'Who?' She asked, baffled.

'Mike Brittle, Ma'am. He says he has news about your car?'

'Oh right.' Claire reached out and the girl handed her the phone.

Claire could hear the man breathing down the handset. 'Hello?'

'Miss Becker, it's Mike from Brittle and Sons in Neilston. I just wanted to give you a quick call to let you know your car is ready to collect.'

'Thank you so much. I'll be there as soon as I can. Can I ask how you knew to find me here?'

Claire heard him shuffle uncomfortably down the line. 'I got a visit from a couple of police officers this morning. They were asking questions about you. I heard about your mother… I'm so sorry to hear about your loss… Anyway, they told me you were staying at Dalmeny Park in Barrhead. I found the number in my phone book.'

Claire paused while she considered this. 'Did I give you my mobile number?' she asked.

'No ma'am. You didn't.'

'Did you not speak to Kieran Grey this morning?'

'No ma'am. I haven't spoken to Mr Grey since yesterday when he was here with you. Is something wrong?'

'No. Everything's fine. Thank you. I'll see you soon.' She handed the receiver back to the girl behind the desk.

'Everything ok, Miss Becker?' she asked, noticing her expression.

Claire flashed her a smile. 'Yes. Fine thanks.'

'Looks like your taxi has arrived,' the girl said, pointing towards the window.

'Thank you.' Claire turned and walked towards the doors. Strange things were happening, and she didn't like it. Somebody was lying to her, but she didn't know who.

***

Claire's taxi stopped outside the Old House Inn. She paid the man and thanked him.

'You don't look too well. You should get more rest,' the driver advised her as he handed her some change.

'Thanks. I will,' she lied, closing the door in his face.

Kieran was early. He sat waiting for her in the same seats where they'd had lunch the day before. She waved at him and walked over.

'I ordered you a vodka Diet Coke,' he said genially.

'Bit early isn't it?' she replied, raising her eyebrows.

'I didn't think you'd care… Also, I figured you could use a drink after the day you had yesterday'

Well, at least on that point he wasn't lying, she thought to herself.

'I like the glasses,' he said, as she took her seat opposite him. 'They make you look like a lawyer.'

'Thanks,' she smiled 'So, what did you find?'

He rummaged in the inside pocket of his jacket and retrieved a small slip of paper. He unfolded it and lay it on the table between them. 'I found another news clipping... I think it might be related to the one we found yesterday.'

Claire picked it up and examined it. There was a picture of some woodland, with a small metal sign peeking out through the grass. The title of the article read, *Discarded Licence Plate Found Belonging to Abandoned Vehicle.'*

'You think this is from the same car?' she asked, staring at the picture.

'Read it,' he urged.

She held the article to her face, squinting through her glasses (the prescription in the lenses was way out of date - she made a mental note to get a new pair).

Police were informed yesterday afternoon of a licence plate found in a wooded area near Uplawmoor, East Renfrewshire. The discarded plate has been confirmed as belonging to a vehicle that was found ten miles away in Montgreenan, in January of this year, nearly eight months ago. With this new information, police have managed to identify the registered owner of the vehicle as one Alice Doyle, 23, of Barrhead. A search is now underway for a body, as police fear the worst; but are refusing to comment at this stage as to whether they suspect foul play might be involved. Police are urging anyone with information regarding Miss Doyle to come forward.

Claire lay the news clipping on the table and leaned back in her chair. Maybe this was it...? Maybe this was the big secret they'd all been hiding for so long.

'Wait,' Kieran said, reaching into the inside pocket of his jacket again. 'There's more...'

He lay another news clipping on the table and Claire stared at it in disbelief.

Body of Missing Woman, Alice Doyle, 23, Found in Woodland

The article was dated 13th September 1998 – nine months after the vehicle had been found.

Police have confirmed that they have found the remains of Alice Doyle, 23, of Barrhead. The body was discovered by a stream at the bottom of a narrow ravine, which rescuers had to use specialist equipment to navigate. The body was initially spotted by police on Thursday afternoon while searching the area, but it took until Friday morning before they were able to reach the body. Miss Doyle's family have been informed of the discovery but declined to comment on the news.

The picture above the article was of a young woman. She was pretty, with long straight blonde hair falling over her eyes. Claire stared at the picture and felt empty inside. Who could do this to such a young girl?

'Well?' Kieran asked, waiting for her reaction. 'Do you think this might have something to do with your parents or not?'

'I don't know,' she replied honesty. 'Maybe… What should we do?'

'Well, I was thinking we might take a drive out to where they found the car. I think I know where it is - I drive past the Montgreenan Estate fairly regularly.'

'That sounds like a good idea.'

'Do you want to finish your drink?' he asked, eyeing her full glass.

'No, just leave it. Come on, let's go.'

Chapter 11
Montgreenan

Kieran had the black Land Rover parked across the street. Claire jumped in the passenger side as he started the engine. Five minutes later they were speeding along country roads towards Uplawmoor – the place where the licence plate had been found. Claire watched the trees pass through the window, picturing the ravine that must be somewhere nearby. How had she gotten to the bottom of that ravine anyway? Was she thrown? Or did she fall down there? Maybe she'd been trying to escape? There were so many unanswered questions.

'Were there anymore news articles?'

'Not that I could find. But I only checked in the months following the discovery of the body. It's possible there's more at some later date.'

'Did you check the internet?' Claire asked.

'No.'

Claire pulled out her phone from her coat pocket and saw the battery was low.

'Shit. My phone's almost dead…'

'It's ok. We can check when we get back.'

Claire stashed the phone back in her pocket. 'It was out there somewhere, wasn't it?' she said.

Kieran looked out towards the woods. 'Yes. Not far from here I think,' he replied.

'What do you think happened to her?'

'I'm not sure... But whatever it was, it wasn't pretty.'

They passed a small sign beside the road that said 'Welcome to Uplawmoor' hidden under a splattering of graffiti. The wall in her mother's bedroom flashed before her eyes; 'Killer', it said, in chaotic red spray paint that had an uncanny resemblance to blood. She winced and tried to wipe the imagine from her mind.

'Everything ok?' Kieran asked.

'Yes, I'm fine,' she lied, rubbing her temples with her thumbs. A police car went screaming passed in the opposite direction and Claire wondered what had happened. 'A bit late now,' she thought idly, watching the lights disappear into the distance.

Five minutes later they were entering Montgreenan – a large estate, not far from the Parish of Kilwinning. Montgreenan House sat at the centre of the estate; a Georgian mansion built in 1817 by Sir Robert Glasgow who had made his fortune in the shipping industry. Montgreenan House was home to the Viscounts Weir until 1982, before it was sold and converted into a hotel. Claire had never stayed in the hotel, but she's passed it as a child and remembered how lavish it had looked.

Her mother had once told her a story about the estate, which she called 'The Lady in the Peat.' The story, which was more of an old wives' tale really and which

Claire still remembered, was about a doctor who had come across a man cutting peats. The man who was usually a dour, unfriendly sort of fellow, had seemed uncharacteristically chipper to the doctor. He told the doctor that there was something he 'had' to show him and proceeded to take him to the long dead corpse of a *bonnie young lassie'* lying in a hole in the peat. The girl, who must have been no older than twenty, had rosy cheeks, blonde hair and a sweet smile playing around her lips. The doctor, needless to say, had been stunned by the discovery and reported it to the authorities of the day. The story goes that the identity of the *Lady in the peat'* was never revealed to the public, although rumours at the time linked her to the family who lived in the Montgreenan Estate.

Claire, recalling the old wives' tale as Kieran took the turn-off into Montgreenan, couldn't help but see the similarities to the story they'd discovered in the news clippings. Both girls had been young and attractive, and both had blonde hair. Both had been discovered, long dead in the woods around Montgreenan Estate, and both stories contained an element of mystery as to how exactly the girls had died. No matter how much of it was truth and how much of it was tale, one thing was for certain, and that was that the Montgreenan Estate was somewhere Claire had some serious reservations about entering.

As Kieran drove the Land Rover through the gates of the Estate, Claire turned to him in disbelief.

'We're going into the estate?' she asked, bewildered.

'Yes,' he replied, navigating the Land Rover over the first set of speed bumps. 'I think this is where they found the car. On one of these backroads inside the estate.'

Claire considered this. The car in the photograph had been in noticeably bad condition. The back had been smashed and there had been blood on the dashboard and steering wheel. *Why would Alice Doyle be driving so fast on these backroads?* They were barely more than a few metres wide and twisted and turned like snakes around the estate; not to mention all the speedbumps that'd been installed every fifty yards with the specific intention of slowing drivers down.

The road towards Montgreenan House was overshadowed by two long lines of overhanging trees. The Estate had been kept in tip-top condition - clearly the effort of a small army of gardeners who worked long hours to keep it looking presentable. Right now, which was still the ends of summer, the hotel would likely be experiencing its busy season and would be operating at near, if not full, capacity. That meant, at this time of year, these small backroads were likely well-travelled; however, in January, in the dead of winter and the midst of a monumental snowstorm, the roads likely saw little to no traffic at all.

So how had it been that Alice Doyle had found herself driving these roads on the night that she'd crashed? Was she working at the hotel, perhaps? A maid, possibly, or waitress in the restaurant? Had she finished her shift then gotten in her car to drive home, only to crash unexpectedly into a tree a few minutes later? But that didn't explain the damage to the back of the vehicle. It was as if someone had crashed into the back of her after she'd crashed into the tree. But there had been no other abandoned vehicles in the paper. The evidence seemed to point to a hit and run, with Alice the unsuspecting victim.

'Over there,' Kieran said, pointing to the turn up ahead and interrupting Claire's chain of thought. It certainly looked familiar, although the wildlife had grown significantly denser than in the picture.

'How do you know?' she asked.

'Because of that milestone,' he replied, motioning to the stone that was stood in the grass. 'There's a lot of milestones around here and that one just happens to have the same thing written on it as the one in the picture.'

'Oh really?' Claire asked.

'I didn't notice it at first as I'd been focusing on the car, but after we'd left the police station that night and you went back to your hotel, I had another look at the news clipping and recognised the milestone as one from Montgreenan almost immediately. They're quite distinctive - See? That one say's *Dundonald ¼ Troon 5 !*' He pointed to the almost illegible lettering on the faded old stone.

'Is that what it says?'

'Yes,' he smiled. He pulled up the Land Rover a few metres from the turn and they both got out.

'That tree there. See it?' He said, pointing at the turn as they made their way towards it. 'That's the tree from the photo, I'm sure of it. That's the tree the car had crashed into in the picture. This is where it happened...' He pulled out the folded news clipping from his breast pocket and handed it to Claire, who unfolded the paper and held it to her face. The tree in the picture was covered in snow, but she recognised the milestone behind the car and the bushes around about it.

'I think your right,' she said, almost excited. 'This is where is happened! Where was she going, do you think?'

'Who knows,' he shrugged. 'Maybe she worked at the hotel?'

'That's what I thought. It makes sense, I guess. But what happened to the *back* of the car?'

'I think if we find that out, we'd be well on our way to finding out what happened to her.'

'You mean if the police never did?'

He nodded. 'Look,' he said, walking towards the tree trunk. 'There on the tree. Can you see it?'

Claire moved closer and looked where he was pointing. There was a small dent in the side of the tree - one suspiciously high enough from the ground to be just about bumper level. The mark had long since healed and the tree had grown around it, but there was definitely a mark there.

Claire brushed it with her finger, 'do you think that's where it hit?'

Kieran nodded. 'I think that's about as much proof as we're going to get. It's been ten years, after all, since the accident, and trees have a way of healing themselves over time.'

'So how did she get from here - from the wrecked car - to the ravine that they'd found her in? That must be miles away from here,' she said, looking around.

'Maybe a mile,' Kieran shrugged. 'The Montgreenan Estate covers all these woodlands around here and about two miles in that direction as well.'

'They own all that land?' Claire asked, amazed.

'Well, at one time they did. I suspect the hotel's handed over care of the land to the Scottish Forestry Commission by now. But at one time, all of that would have been Montgreenan land.'

Claire stood up and straightened herself out, stashing the folded news clipping in the pocket of her jeans. 'What now?' she asked.

'Well…' he shrugged. 'Fancy a walk?'

Chapter 12
Lead Feathers

Kieran led Claire along the winding back roads of the estate, until they came across a stile in the fencing. Kieran hopped over first, then held out his hand to help Claire over after him. Now they were surrounded by fresh woodland, clear of the boundaries of the hotel.

'Which way?' Claire asked.

'Over here, I think,' Kieran replied, finding a small path that twisted between the trees.

They followed the path through the woods until it led them up a small hillock. Claire turned and saw the whole Montgreenan Estate laid out beneath them. It looked lush and green, with the old mansion house at its centre.

'You know, I remember driving past this place as a kid. My mother would tell me stories about *'The Lady in the Peat'*.'

Kieran turned to look at her. 'I know the story,' he replied.

They walked on for another fifteen minutes or so, as the path led them deeper into the woods. Most of the trees that they passed were either dead or not long for this world. The woods felt old and neglected; void of life except for the chirping in the branches above them. Eventually they came across a small stream which meandered parallel to their footpath. They followed the stream as it grew steadily into a burn, flowing some six feet wide beside the path. As the stream grew, the path began an incline, creating a small drop-off to their side that was becoming increasingly precipitous.

As they climbed further up the hill, the drop-off had become a cliff edge. There was no fence or protective barrier separating the footpath where they walked from the perilous drop that was right beside them.

'Do you think that's it?' Claire asked, moving closer and peering over the edge. She could just about make out the river running at the bottom. The tops of the trees growing alongside the river were just about at eye-level to where they were walking – one hundred feet separating them from the bottom. 'Where they found her?'

Kieran joined her along the edge, staring out through the treetops towards the river. 'Could be,' he mused.

They walked further, with the path skirting the cliff edge; all the while glimpsing sparks of light from the river, as the sun danced between the trees and reflected off the surface. The clouds overhead were starting to dissipate and scatter, leaving the sun to

beam down on them from a brilliant blue sky. Claire
undid her jacket and threw it over her shoulder. Years
of smoking (that she'd since replaced with puffing on
nicotine inhalers) and imbibing more alcohol than she
cared to remember, had left her somewhat out of
shape; at least internally. Externally she was still as
lean as she'd been as a teenager at her first high school
dance - a size six and proud of it - though it wasn't
through exercise and proper diet that she'd maintained
her slim figure.

Kieran, on the other hand, still had his bodywarmer fastened to his neckline. It was clear to Claire,
that he'd taken a lot better care of his body than she
had of hers. But what exactly did he do with his time
when he wasn't spending it with her? He clearly didn't
tend the fields or do the other work that needed doing
around his property, judging by the clear deterioration
it had undergone since the death of his parents. So,
what was it that he did? Other than a collector of
course (as if that could be a profession). Was he that
rich that all he had to do with his time was
scour through old news articles and paste the ones he
felt like keeping into scrapbooks? Surely that couldn't
be the case. The way he lived, in the shabby back
building of his parent's rundown farmhouse, was a
clear indication that he was just about scraping the
bottom of the barrel. Although the car he drove
around in did seem to suggest otherwise.

The man was a mystery to Claire - one she
couldn't help but dwell on. His quiet demeanour and
handsome exterior certainly made matters easier and
went some way to dissuading her from asking the real

questions that were troubling her. Behind that stoic and obliging facade, she couldn't help but feel that the man was lying to her.

'Over there!' he said suddenly, pointing to the trees down near the river.

Claire looked up and almost tripped over a tree root that protruded from the earth.

'Where?' she said, finding her balance on his shoulder.

Kieran grabbed her arm and pointed at a place down below them, through the trees and dancing sunlight to the river shore at the bottom. There, next to the water tied neatly to a tree and hidden from the world above them, were flowers.

'You see them?' he asked, directing her eyes with his finger.

Claire nodded slowly before the realisation hit home.

'That's it!' she cried, sending a bird into flight above them. 'That's where they found her!'

***

Over ten years on from the tragic events that caused the untimely demise of Alice Doyle, someone had still found the penitence to climb down the gorge-side and pay their respects at the place where her body had been found.

'Who do you think left them?' Claire asked, leaning over the ledge as far as she could go, and using a branch to keep from toppling.

'Family maybe? Or perhaps someone who knows something that the police never unearthed...'

'You think whoever crashed into the back of her did this?'

'It's possible...' he admitted.

'D'you think there's a note?'

'Do you want to climb down and find out?'

'Not really...' she admitted, feeling slightly sick at the prospect.

'Whoever left those flowers must have been here before...' Kieran mused. 'It would take a decent amount of gear to get down there unscathed. Unless of course they went down the river - maybe a kayak? Who knows...?'

'I wonder how she ended up there...?' Claire found herself wondering again. 'It's a long way to fall.'

'It sure is...'

Claire's phone vibrated in her pocket, surprising her. She pulled it out and examined it.

'I thought your battery was dead?'

'So did I... Seems I'm on my last two percent.'

'Who is it?' Kieran asked.

'Missed call. I don't recognise the number. Could be work.'

'Or the police? They did say you'd be needed for further questioning.'

This was true. Claire saw the painful image flash before her eyes once again. Her mother's body on the mattress. Sheets pulled to one side. *Killer'* written accusingly in red paint.

'Claire?' Kieran asked, breaking her from her daydream.

'Yes, the police. I'd forgotten. We better get back so I can call them.'

***

Kieran pulled the Land Rover into a Brittle & Sons parking bay.

'I'll meet you back at the hotel,' she said, closing the door behind her.

Mike rolled himself out from under a car when he heard the footsteps approaching. He picked himself up and rubbed the oil from his gloves on the side of his overalls. 'Miss Becker! I've got your car waiting for you out back. I was so sorry to hear of your loss - you look well, considering the circumstances... Tragic thing, losing a loved one. I lost my own mother a few years back – it was the cancer that got her in the end. Are you doing ok?'

'I'm fine thanks,' she smiled, pulling her purse out from her bag. 'How much do I owe you?'

'Oh, seventy-five pounds should do it.'

'Do you take card?' She asked, flashing her Visa Debit.

'Sure. Come inside. I'll ring you up and get you your keys.'

Inside his office, Mike handed Claire the card reader and she quickly entered her pin. As she did so, a random thought crossed her mind.

'Mike?' she asked. 'How long have you been in Neilston?'

Mike handed her the keys and stashed the card reader back beneath the desk. 'Well, we opened up this place ten years back and before that I worked at the Keeble MOT Repair Shop in Barrhead. And before that —'

'So, you've been in the area for a while then?' Claire interrupted.

'Yes, I guess you could say that,' he said over his shoulder as he turned to stash a folder back in the filing cabinet behind him

'Well... forgive me for asking, but do you ever remember hearing about a girl found at the bottom of ravine near the Montgreenan estate?'

Mike stopped what he was doing and turned back to face her - his brows were furrowed, and he had a curious look in his eye. 'You mean the Doyle girl,' he said. 'Sure, I remember her. Long time ago now. They found her car all bashed 'n' beaten on that big estate. Why d'you ask?'

Claire shifted awkwardly on her feet. 'I was just wondering, what you knew about what happened to her?'

'Nobody knows what happened to her, that's the story isn't it? Police report said she died from falling down that ravine in those woods - but if you ask me, I'd say there's more to it than that.'

'Like somebody was chasing her?' Claire asked.

'Or somebody pushed her...' He slammed the drawer of the filing cabinet shut and sat himself in the chair behind his desk. 'But that's just an old man talking. Its case closed, as they say. Nobody's mentioned that girl in a long time.'

'So, they never arrested anybody?'

'Nope. Doubt they ever will either. Too long ago now. People move on. They forget.'

'Did she have a family?'

Mike folded his fingers and stared up at her curiously. 'This is a strange thing to be talking about, isn't it? We should be talking about your mother, if we're going to talk at all.'

Claire felt herself blush and shifted uncomfortably on her feet again. 'It doesn't matter,' she said, awkwardly. 'I was just curious. I'll let you get back to work.' She turned to leave and reached for the door handle.

'She had a mother,' Mike called to her, just as she was just about to leave. 'Died a few years back. She's buried over in the cemetery at the edge of town. Next to her daughter... I think.'

**

Back at the hotel, Claire drove her newly fixed car into the parking space alongside the black Land Rover. Kieran was stood casually waiting beside it.

'D'you want me to wait?' he asked.

'No, you should come. We can check the internet for any more news on Alice Doyle - if there ever was any more news.'

'Ok.'

They left the cars and made their way through the entrance of the Dalmeny Park Hotel. The girl at reception smiled as they approached.

'Good afternoon,' she said warmly.

'I was wondering if I'd received any messages?' Claire asked, returning the girl's smile.

'One moment please, I'll check.' She spun in her chair to her computer screen. 'Miss Becker, one message received at one o'clock today from Constable Morgan at the Neilston Police Station. Would you like me to read it?'

'No thanks,' Claire replied. 'Did she leave a number?'

'She did. One moment and I'll write it down for you.' She grabbed a notepad and a pen then scribbled down the number and handed the note to Claire.

'Thank you. Could I possibly use your phone?' she asked.

'There's a pay phone over there,' she said, pointing towards the lobby. 'It takes card if you don't have any change.'

'Thank you,' Claire replied, slightly perturbed.

The girl smiled and returned to her computer screen. Claire pulled out her purse and searched for some change. She found a pound coin and slotted it into the pay phone. Dialling the number on the note, she waited as it rang.

'Neilston Station,' came a voice from the other end.

'Oh hello, I've had a message from Constable Morgan. I was wondering if she was available?'

'Who's calling please?'

'My name's Claire Becker.'

'Oh, Miss Becker, we've been expecting your call.'

The line went quiet for a second, as the person on the other end fumbled with the handset.

'Miss Becker, this is Chief Inspector Pommery. We need you to come into the station immediately. How soon can you get here?'

'I can be there in thirty minutes,' Claire replied, glancing up at Kieran, who was stood beside her.

'Good… And Miss Becker, it's important you come alone. Do you understand?'

'Yes, I understand.'

'Good. I will see you within the hour then. Goodbye.' He hung up the phone.

Claire turned to Kieran, still holding the receiver against her chest. 'Well? What did they say?' he asked.

'They want me to come to the station.'

'Okay. Let's go. I'll drive you.' Kieran turned to leave.

'Wait… They want me to go alone…'

'Alone? Why?'

'They didn't say. Just that it was important I came alone.'

Kieran stared at her intently. His eyes boring holes into hers. 'Fine,' he said finally. 'Call me when you're done. I can wait here.'

'Actually, it's probably best you just go back to your place for now. I need to sort a few things out with the funeral etcetera. There's so much to be done and I'm the only one left to do it.'

'Of course. I understand. Well… I'll see you later then I guess.' He smiled at her and turned to leave.

'Wait!' she called, feeling guilty for the somewhat cold dismissal. 'I just wanted to say… thank you… for helping me these past few days. I appreciate it.'

'No problem,' he nodded. And with that, he was gone.

Chapter 13
The Chief

Neilston Police Station was located at the far edge of town near the J&M Murdoch textile factory. Once the proud employer of over a third of the town's population, the factory now operated as more of a warehouse than a steaming titan of industry. The J&M building itself was one of the oldest mill structures left standing in Scotland, with a history dating back to 1792. It was one of the seven large mills along the banks of the river Levern, which runs between Neilston and Dovecothall.

The police station, scanty in comparison, lay directly across the street from the factory. Claire parked her small pale blue Fiat 500 in one of the four parking spaces to the rear of the building and made her way around to the entrance. The officer behind the desk was a round woman whose hat was dwarfed by her somewhat bulbous head. Claire approached the bench and parked herself in front of it.

'Excuse me.'

The round woman didn't bother looking up. She seemed to be working her way through a packet of Real McCoy crisps that had salted her fingers and the keyboard in front of her.

'Excuse me,' she tried again. 'My name is Claire Becker, I'm here by request of Chief Inspector Pommery.'

The round woman stopped eating and looked up at her. She turned in her chair and hit a button behind her. Five seconds later, a tall man with a bushy grey moustache marched out of a room to her left and introduced himself.

'Ah, Miss Becker. I'm Chief Inspector Pommery. Thank you for coming on such short notice. If you would please follow me.' He walked back through the door that led to the room to their left and Claire followed dutifully behind him. The room was a large office where several police officers were sat behind workstations - some of them taking calls and some of them chatting. They all looked up and stopped talking at once when Claire and the man entered. Chief Inspector Pommery led her to the back of the large office and into a small interview room that was equipped with a table and two chairs.

'Take a seat please,' he said, lowering himself into the chair opposite. 'Miss Becker, once again I would just like to offer you my condolences. This must be a very difficult time for you, and I understand this is probably the last place you want to be right now, with funeral arrangements and such to be dealt with.'

Claire nodded, then found herself asking, 'Pommery – like the champagne?'

'As a matter of fact, I do,' he replied, looking rather amused by the question. He paused for a second, as if he'd lost his train of thought, before he started up again. 'Oh yes, the matter of your mother. We are terribly sorry to be taking up your time, however, I must admit, I am extremely glad that we managed to get a hold of you on such short notice.'

He edged himself closer. 'I'm afraid the man who you've been spending your time with, since your arrival back in Neilston, may not be who he says he is…'

'Excuse me?'

'*Kieran Grey*, I believe, is the name that he's been using. We checked him out this morning and could find no record of anybody living in the Grey farm since the deaths of the previous owners, Lawrence and Joyce Grey, within one week of each other, in August ninety-nine. There is no record of any children, or any next of kin for that matter, which is why the farm has remained abandoned since the death of its tenants. Since no next of kin could be found, after an exhaustive search I might add, the estate fell into the possession of the East Renfrewshire Council, nearly ten years ago.'

Claire's mouth fell open as her eyes darted between the police officer's and the table.

'You mean… that isn't Kieran Grey?'

'We don't know his name, unfortunately. We've been trying to conduct a trace of when exactly he began squatting in the farm building and why it went unnoticed for so long - but so far we've had little success.'

Claire tried to process what she'd heard, but her mind was struggling to make sense of it.

'But... But... Who is he then?' she stuttered.

'As soon as we find that out, Miss Becker, we will let you know, but until that time, we suggest you stay as far away from him as possible. We have two officers in a car at this very moment with a warrant for his arrest. Squatting in a residential building is a serious offence and won't be taken lightly. We are hoping that once we have him in custody, more details will come to light about who he is, and why exactly he's been lying.'

'D'you think he... killed my mother?' she whispered, raising her hand to her mouth and staring at him in panic.

'There is no evidence of that, as of yet. We have the forensic team at the scene, and any evidence they find will be analysed fully before making any arrests.'

Claire could feel herself starting to crack. She'd done her best to hold herself together, but her world seemed to be crumbling down around her once again.

'Miss Becker? Are you ok?'

'I'm fine,' she lied, forcing herself to smile.

'If there's anything you need, we're happy to help. We have a psychologist on staff who would be happy to talk to you, if you like?'

'No thank you. I'm fine.'

'Very well. In that case, I must insist that you stay as far away from this man as possible, and once again, it's probably best if you don't leave the area. We may need to bring you back in again, should anything come to light.'

'Of course,' she said, rising from her chair. Chief Inspector Pommery led her to the door and back out to the reception. The police officers at their desks all stared as she walked by.

'One more thing, before you go,' he said, holding the entrance door open for her. 'It occurred to me that you might not have had the best relationship with your mother.'

'That's one way of putting it,' Claire replied, wryly.

'Well, with that said, I was just wondering if you knew of any enemies that your parents may have made over the years? You might not know this, but it came to our attention some time ago that someone had been vandalising the grave of your father. When we investigated this, we found it was in fact your mother who had been cleaning the graffiti from the headstone – sometimes as often as once a month she'd be up there with a bucket and sponge, scrubbing the stone clean. Were you aware of this?'

'No,' Claire lied, looking away quickly. 'I didn't know. And as for the enemies, she could have had any number that I wouldn't know about – she hasn't been in my life for a very long time.'

'That's a shame… Family is so important – especially in times like these. Anyway, I will let you get on. You remember what I said about Mr Grey? Stay well away.'

'I will,' she lied again.

Sat back in her car, Claire found her phone in her handbag. She typed three single words and hit send. *Where are you?*

Chapter 14
Bagram

Claire's phone vibrated in her handbag as she was driving. Wherever 'Kieran Grey' was, she was going to find him immediately. She pulled over to the curb and grabbed her phone from her bag. The text was from Kieran – *'I'm back at the farm. What did the police say?'*

She quickly typed her reply and hit send – *'Stay where you are. I'm coming over.'*

She took the next turn, towards Kingston Road. *This fucker is going to come clean to me now. He's not getting away this time,* she thought, as she pressed her foot down on the accelerator. She took the turn-off at Station Road that led out onto Main Street. She was less than five minutes away when her phone started vibrating again. She reached over a hand and dug the phone out from inside her bag – her screen showed an incoming call from a number she didn't recognise – it wasn't local.

Claire held the phone to her ear with her shoulder, 'Hello?'

'Claire, are you there? It's me, Noah.'

'Oh Noah, thank God! Where are you?'

'What's going on? I heard the news... about mum. They're saying something about writing on the walls... What are they talking about? Hello? Can you hear me?'

'Yes, I can still hear you. Where are you? Can you get here?'

'I'm at the airfield in Bagram. I'm shipping back to the UK tonight. I managed to hitch a lift with Charlie Company – they're due to roll off.'

'Can you get here?'

'Yes, I'll be there as soon as I can. Claire, what's going on? They're saying she was murdered?'

'I don't know what's happening,' she could feel herself starting to well up. 'I need help...'

'I'll be there as soon as I can,' he repeated. 'And Claire? Take care, ok?'

'I will. See you soon.' She hung up the phone and threw it back on the passenger seat.

A police car sped by her in the opposite direction – lights and siren both wailing in flashes of noise and colour. She eased her foot on the pedal automatically, and the car slowed back down to thirty. It was starting to get dark again - the streetlamps flickered on around her as the daylight diminished. *I have to get to that house before the police take him*, she thought. She considered sending him another text to warm him but thought better of it. *Maybe he should be taken into custody? After all, who is he really? And why is he here? For all I know he's the one who wrote that shit across the wall...* Claire slammed her foot on the brake and the car skidded to a stop. In her distraction she'd driven clear through a

Stop junction and the van driver, who'd had to perform an emergency brake to avoid hitting her, was yelling obscenities through his windshield.

'Why don't you watch where you're fucking going, you bitch!' he roared, as Claire's racing heart sank slowly back to her chest. This wasn't like her at all... She wasn't thinking clearly. She needed a drink to clear her head and calm herself down. *Don't be an idiot, there's no time for that!* she thought, furious at the notion.

She drove the rest of the way to the farm as slowly as possible – driving the way a drunk person would when they think that by being overly careful it makes up for the fact that they shouldn't be behind the wheel. As she approached the farm, she saw that she was already too late – two police cars were pulled up on the pebbled drive of the Grey farm, and one of them had noticed her approach and was pointing in her direction.

Claire threw the car into reverse and sped backwards down the road, performing a crudely executed J-turn when she felt the tyres leaving the gravel. She raced back down the road towards town. In her rear-view mirror she could see that the police hadn't followed her. She breathed deeply through her nose and thought about what she would do next.

Chapter 15
A Crow Left of the Murder

Chief Inspector Pommery hung up the phone and breathed a deep sigh of satisfaction. He'd just received a call from his dispatch informing him that Officers Ward and Nicol had just taken the man claiming to be Kieran Grey into custody. Soon he would walk through the front door of this very station and be greeted by the Chief Inspector himself. Then be led away to an interview room to commence, what would likely be, a full night of questioning.

Pommery didn't mind. He was long accustomed to working all hours of the night, and his wife and grown daughter were accustomed to it too. He'd been in the police force now for nearly thirty-five years, starting on the day after his twenty-fourth birthday - he remembered that day well.

Back then he'd been nothing but a 'beat cop', as their friends across the pond called them, working the streets of Govan in Glasgow, and reporting to a man whose funeral he'd attended nearly ten years ago. Thirty-five years in the police force is enough to make anyone's retirement seem inviting, and he was a mere three years away from that final milestone.

The average length of service for your run-of-the-mill Chief Inspector ranged from ten years to fifteen years, and this was his fourteenth year wearing those three diamond brooches on his shoulder. He reported to one man and one man only within the Southern Glasgow district, and that was the superintendent, who would likely be taking his own retirement any day soon.

He'd been working out of Neilston for nearly twenty-two years, since he'd moved there with his wife and daughter Sarah, when she was just a girl, in search of something a little less hectic than the rampant streets of Glasgow. Neilston was rural territory and far enough from the big city that its nights were mostly quiet, and its streets were mostly clean. On most weeks, he would only need to drive through to Glasgow just the once to visit the Sheriff Court - usually on a Friday. His days of testifying in trials were behind him but he accompanied some of the junior officers, to make sure everything stayed in order. Order... a word Bill Pommery held in the highest regards and a concept that he'd been striving to achieve since he first buttoned up his blue and black uniform. Neilston had order and that was something that allowed him to sleep peacefully most nights - until the day came when he handed back the gun and his badge, but he would worry about that when it came to it.

Bill Pommery heard the cars arriving in front of the station before the doors had even been opened.

There had been no sirens at that point (likely cut-off once they'd left the centre of town), but Bill had heard the engines of the old BMW estate cars as they pulled up in front of the building. Thirty seconds later, the glass doors swung open and Officer Ward and Officer Nicol strode in behind Mr Grey, who was cuffed behind the back.

Bill pushed back his chair and went to meet them at the front desk. By the time he'd got there the water was already starting to pool beneath their boots. They were shaking their wet hair and ringing their gloves and Mr Grey stood silently behind them, patiently watching. The weather this summer had been the wettest in nearly a decade - it'd been constant rain for as far back as he could remember.

'Well done lads. I take it Mr Grey didn't put up much of a struggle?'

'Docile as a pussy cat this one,' Officer Luke Ward replied. 'Some state that property is in now though. You can barely see the furniture for the piles of papers lying everywhere. We found Mr Grey sat in the back room, examining old newspaper clippings. Came without a fuss. He's one cool customer this one, Chief...'

'Well, we'll see how cool he is after eight hours of questioning. He's bound to crack eventually - they all do.'

Bill Pommery took Kieran by the shoulder and led him through the back. He wanted to get this interview started as promptly as possible, so they had something to give the papers in the morning. It wasn't every day the quiet town of Neilston had a murder like this one.

He was still waiting on the prints and the DNA samples from the crime scene, but as soon as he had them, he fully expected Mr Grey to be a match on both counts.

He turned to Officer Ward. 'Get his prints done and swab him, then we'll get him in interview room two. I want this done quickly.'

'Right you are, sir,' the young Officer replied.

Ten minutes later, Bill Pommery had his fresh coffee on the table and was setting up Interview Room 2, when Officer Ward returned with Mr Grey.

'Come in, please. Take a seat.' he said jovially. The young Officer closed the door behind him and left the two men in the small room alone. Bill had hit the record button on the camera before he'd entered, and the small red light on it blinked at him from the corner.

'Mr Grey, do you understand why you've been arrested?'

Kieran stared back at the elder man calmly. 'I do,' he said.

'And do you realise that we're currently on the hunt for a murder suspect for a victim found not two hundred metres from the house that you've been squatting in?'

'I do,' he said again.

'Well in that case, are you willing to tell me why you've been pretending to be a man you most certainly are not? There's no record of anyone by the name of 'Kieran Grey' ever being born in the area or ever having lived at the house you're illegally inhabiting. What do you say to that?'

Kieran observed the man patiently. 'It was empty when I got there.'

'Well, that doesn't give you the right to just move yourself in, I'm afraid. Do you have any idea how seriously we take the matter of unlawful inhabitation in this country? You could be looking at a sizeable custodial sentence, at the very least!'

Kieran merely blinked at him.

'Can you tell me your real name?'

Kieran blinked. 'My name's Kieran.'

'And your surname?'

Kieran sighed and leaned back in his chair. 'I can't tell you that.'

'And why's that?'

Kieran shrugged.

'Look, Mr Grey, or whatever the hell your name is, you're in some serious trouble here and you're not making this any easier on yourself. And we haven't even got onto the matter of your potential involvement in the murder of one Mrs Gwendolyn Becker.'

'I had nothing to do with that.'

'Well, that's yet to be seen. Initial reports back from the lab suggest that she's been dead for nearly eight weeks. You remain the person in closest proximity to the crime, and you've been lying about your identity... Do you see how this could merit suspicion? The state that poor woman's body had been left in was quite appalling - but I assume you know that already?'

'Do I?'

'Mrs Becker was stabbed through the stomach, causing her, what was likely, an extremely slow and painful death. Do you know what happens to someone when they're stabbed directly through the stomach, Mr Grey? No? Well, believe me, it isn't pleasant. Mrs Becker was unfortunate enough to have the stab wound miss most of her vital organs and major arteries, which would have shortened her suffering considerably. The knife ruptured her stomach lining, causing her gut to leak into her peritoneal cavity. The infection alone would have killed her within a day or two, but this isn't how she died. No, Mrs Gwendolyn Becker likely underwent more suffering than either you or I could possibly imagine. Initial autopsy reports show that her heart and lungs are showing signs of corrosion, meaning the acid from her stomach likely found its way into her chest cavity as well. Can you possibly imagine the extent of suffering that this poor woman underwent before she died?'

'It wasn't me. Like I told you already,' Kieran replied, standing his ground.

'And what about the daughter? What's your interest in her?'

'No interest. Just being neighbourly.'

'And when she finds out you've been lying to her the whole time - what then?'

'Who I am isn't important.'

'It's not? Then please tell me, what is?'

'The truth...'

'What truth?'

'About what really happened that night...'

'And what night would that be, Mr Grey?'

'I think you know...'

'No please, enlighten me. Which night are you referring to?' Pommery urged.

Kieran rested both his hands on the table and leaned ever so slightly closer. 'The night of twenty-fifth of December, nineteen-ninety-seven. Surely you remember? You were there after all...'

Chapter 16
Cold Case

Bill Pommery leaned back in his seat and twisted the ends of his moustache distractedly. *Christmas ninety-seven? But that was that whole mess with the Doyle girl, wasn't it? What does this idiot know about it?* he thought to himself, curiously.

Bill Pommery had indeed been present the day young Miss Doyle's car has been found abandoned, and then again, several months later when her body was found at the bottom of the ravine near the Montgreenan Estate. He'd been Chief Inspector for nearly three years when it happened - the poor, pretty young girl with so much left to live for.

They still had her autopsy addendum on file - she'd succumbed to wounds consistent with a fall; her neck was broken and so was her arm. Yet something about the circumstances didn't strike him as accidental. There had been another car involved of course, that was obvious from the state that her car had been left in. There was even some paint residue scratched onto its rear bumper - they were looking for a red car, or so it seemed. Despite ample investigation and two years of examining evidence, they'd hit a resoundingly dogged brick wall and no charges were ever filed. The case had been filed amongst the cold cases, gathering dust down in the storeroom. He hadn't thought about that case in years. Why was it on the table now?

'The Doyle girl? What's it to you?' he asked, still twisting the twills of his moustache.

'It's everything to me. EVERYTHING,' Kieran repeated.

Bill Pommery straightened up in his chair and observed the man peculiarly. 'Who are you?' he asked, staring intently into his eyes.

'I would have thought you'd've worked that one out by now, Inspector,' Kieran replied, a strange smirk curling on his lips. 'My name is Kieran Doyle...'

***

Chief Inspector Pommery's mouth gradually slid open as his jaw muscles went slack. He didn't say anything for nearly a full minute while he looked the young man up and down, trying to discern if he were lying.

'The brother?' he asked, gripping the side of the table firmly. 'You're the brother?'

Kieran nodded. 'Yes, Inspector... I am. And we've met before…'

Chapter 17
Flashbacks

Kieran Doyle grew up living with his mother and his elder sister in a small, dilapidated bungalow in the roughest part of Barrhead. Alice, eight years his senior, had always been a caring older sister and even more so when she'd stepped up and taken over the main household duties, when their mother, now confined to a wheelchair, had become too sick to work or cook the meals. She'd insisted they didn't need the help of a carer and that she take care of their mother by herself.

Alice's job waitressing at the hotel located on the Montgreenan Estate had kept food on the table and kept the debt collectors from their doorstep. Kieran attended school at St Luke's High School in Barrhead - the same school where his sister had served as Head Girl, some years before. Kieran didn't take to life at school nearly as naturally as Alice had. His teachers believed that he was somewhere on the spectrum (whatever that meant) and that he may have something known as 'Ass Burgers'. Since he never seemed to be able to focus well in class, he found himself skipping school altogether with increasing regularity.

Neither of the Doyle children had many friends. His sister had never had a boyfriend and spent most of her time working at the hotel and taking care of Kieran and their mother. It was a lot of responsibility to take on at such an early age, but she'd never complained once.

Their father had walked out on them long before Kieran was grown. Their mother always said, 'good riddance,' and 'you're better off without him', but Kieran sometimes thought it would've been quite nice to have a man around the house sometimes. He'd never even met him – the man had walked out the door when he was only three months old. Then, when he was thirteen, their mother had been diagnosed with multiple sclerosis. She deteriorated rapidly and was quickly confined to a wheelchair. Quickly they realised that she could only talk a little, and only on her good days, but the things she did say began to make less and less sense, until she could barely string a coherent sentence together. Kieran found it fascinating to watch her go downhill so quickly.

When Christmas came around, Alice saw the opportunity to start pulling double shifts at the hotel. She even worked Christmas Day (they were paying staff double-time for volunteering to work and she couldn't pass up the opportunity). That night, while Kieran had been at home, helping his infirm mother with her dinner, Alice finished her ten-hour shift at the Montgreenan Estate and had gotten into her car to drive herself home and to bed.

The next morning, when Kieran noticed that his sister hadn't returned home, he considered phoning the hotel to ask them if they'd seen her but decided against it. This was highly unusual behaviour for Alice, and Kieran could remember thinking just that. However, there was the remote possibility that maybe she'd stayed with a friend or a boy she'd met at work? She was a grown woman now, after all, and was free to stay out as early or as late as she chose to. When Alice didn't come home the next night, after her Boxing Day shift had ended, Kieran began to worry. He toyed with the idea of phoning the police station over on Cathcart Street and reporting her missing. For some reason, he chose not to.

Maybe it was because he was only fifteen at the time and was still very much the shy and awkward teenager that he'd been up until then. Or maybe it was because he still expected his sister to show up at any moment, heaving along bags from the supermarket and telling him to '*get mum ready for dinner.*' Or maybe it was because speaking it out loud would cement it into reality as something that was actually happening, and not just in his head.

The next day, Kieran decided to walk himself into town and pick up some food, since the fridge was nearly empty. On the way, he passed by the newsagents that he called 'Mo's' (but it was actually called 'Mina's'). This was the first time he saw the news clipping that would change his life forever.

'*Abandoned Car Found.*'

He grabbed the paper and examined the car on the cover. It was Alice's car, he had little doubt about that. He could even see her bergamot scented air fresher hanging from the rear-view mirror (a smell she said reminded her of Earl Grey tea, which she'd drank since she was little). For some reason, that he couldn't understand, he noticed that the licence plate had been torn from the back of her car - it was missing.

He took the paper from the stand, without paying, and ran all the way home with it tucked under his arm. When he got in, his mother was sitting in the front room in her chair facing the television; but she wasn't really watching it, he knew. Her graze had drifted slightly left towards the window and he suspected she was dreaming about being able to roam outside again. He put the paper on the small coffee table and read the article in full.

Once he was finished, he walked over to the kitchen, grabbed the phone from the wall and dialled '101' - Barrhead Police Station.

'Barrhead station,' came the voice from the other end.

Kieran hesitated, then hung up the receiver in a panic. His heart raced maniacally, and he slumped against the wall. What was wrong with him? Why couldn't he do it? It was a bizarre feeling but phoning the police station would somehow cement the situation in his mind; that his sister was in fact missing and that was in fact her battered car in the paper on the table. The prospect of this seemed too much for him to handle. It overwhelmed him - he felt useless. He dropped the phone, letting it bounce and dangle on its plastic springy chord, then slid to the floor and cried like a baby.

Days went by, weeks, and Kieran would walk past the newsagents and collect the local paper, The Barrhead Courier. He watched for any articles on the car they'd found abandoned, but no more news came. He supposed he was in denial... Instead of throwing the papers away, he started stockpiling them in the dining room behind the table. After a month, he'd collected a pile of thirty papers and counting.

The phone rang occasionally in the beginning but got less frequent as the time passed. He assumed it would be Alice's work asking where she was and why she hadn't shown up for her shift that evening. He wondered why the hotel hadn't connected the dots by now: abandoned car in the paper; girl not turning up for work. Surely someone she worked with would know what her car looked like and had seen it in the paper? Not to mention the fact that the car itself had been found on the Montgreenan Estate. It was all so strange. He couldn't make any sense of it.

As the months went slowly by, their mother started to notice something missing - although she couldn't express it in a way that was coherent. 'Argba,' she'd say. 'Argba... arghba, arghbaaa.'

He knew what that meant but didn't have the fortitude to explain it to her. As the papers piled higher and any chance of her walking through the door again grew bleaker, Kieran became numb to whole situation. The house he lived in had turned into a trash heap. Dirty plates were everywhere, and some had started to grow mould on them in the sink. He could tell his mother was getting worse when he attempted to wash her, but he couldn't think of anything practical to do about it.

When September came, so did the news.

'Body Found in Ravine.'

The article included a brief interview with Chief Inspector Pommery of the Neilston police, whose team had made the discovery. There was a small picture of a greying man with a large moustache, dressed in a white shirt, black tie and a checkered policeman's helmet.

His first instinct after reading the article was to get out the scissors and add the cut-out to the scrapbook he'd been assembling. During the months he'd amassed clippings, there'd been no news on his sister, but there had been plenty of other missing people in the area: a woman, 45, from Dreghorn, near Irvine, missing for two weeks then discovered down in England with a man she'd left her husband for; another woman, 59, missing for three weeks from Eaglesham, south of Glasgow, found living in a flat she used to own in the seventies with the man who was currently renting the place. A boy, 15, from the Isle of Arran, found living in a cave near the beach, two miles from his home (it turned out he'd murdered a four-year-old girl). The rate people were disappearing in the central belt of Scotland was becoming endemic.

Kieran collected the clippings hungrily, finding with each new entry in the scrapbook, a small piece of him was filled in the place where Alice had once been.

Lately, the phone had begun ringing off the hook. It went strangely frequently and though he hadn't answered it in months, he was becoming increasingly tempted by the ringing. Eventually, one day in mid-September, a man arrived at their door. It was Chief Inspector Pommery from the newspaper article - Kieran recognised him immediately.

As the doorbell chimed, his mother started to yelp. He wheeled her into the kitchen and hid her behind the table. The doorbell chimed again, and Kieran crept towards the window and peered between the blinds. The Chief Inspector was on the doorstep, his hat held under his armpit.

When the bell chimed a third time, Kieran's mother shrieked from the kitchen.

'Hello?' came a gruff voice from behind the door. 'Is anybody in there?'

Kieran jerked around at the sound of his mother. Pommery saw the movement behind the window and walked over the grass for a closer look. He placed his hand flat on the glass and looked inside.

'Excuse me? Ma'am, are you there? I'm with the Neilston Police Department. I need to talk to you about your daughter.'

Kieran cringed. *Shit!* He'd been seen.

'Ma'am? Police. Would you open the door please?'

Kieran bit his lower lip in frustration, then quietly and timidly crept towards the front door. He turned the lock slowly and opened it just wide enough for a single beam of daylight to cut across the carpet.

'Yes?' he whispered through the gap.

'Sir? My name is Chief Inspector Pommery. This is regarding a Miss Alice Doyle. Do you happen to know her whereabouts?'

Kieran opened the door another inch. 'You found Alice?' he asked quietly.

'Are you aware that Miss Doyle was never reported missing? I take it from your reaction that you haven't seen her in quite some time. Is that correct?'

'She's been gone...' Kieran replied, timidly.

'If it's ok with you. I would like to come inside and ask you and your mother some questions. Can you open the door?'

Kieran hesitated then opened the door fully, sending a flooding of daylight into the dark room behind him.

'I won't take up too much of your time,' Pommery said, stamping his boots on the mat, then walking through the threshold. Kieran led him to the living room which hadn't been cleaned or tidied in several months. He grabbed the dirty dishes from the coffee table and took them through to the kitchen, where his mother was whining. He left the dishes by the sink, then wheeled his mother back through to the room with him, where Pommery was waiting.

Pommery was tall, with a thick greying patch of hair and a particularly bushy moustache that, along with his eyebrows, resembled three overgrown caterpillars crawling across his face. Both of them took a seat on the couch and Pommery placed his hat on the table.

'I apologise, ma'am,' he said to Kieran's mother. 'I didn't realise that... well... you'd require assistance.'

Kieran's mother wasn't looking. She had slid down in her chair and was craning her neck to the window. Pommery turned to Kieran. 'This is the current and most recent residence of Miss Alice Doyle, is that correct?'

Kieran nodded.

'I'm afraid I have some rather troubling news regarding your sister...' He folded his hands on his lap, solemnly. 'We recently discovered a body not far from the hotel where Miss Doyle was known to have worked. The hotel manager, Mr Kelso, has told police that Miss Doyle hasn't shown up for work in several months, and that she didn't leave any formal communication to say that she would be taking an extended leave of absence.'

'Is she dead?' Kieran asked, curiously.

Pommery observed him peculiarly - as if the question had been one as inane as one about the weather. 'We have not, as of yet, identified the remains. Actually, that's one of the reasons that I'm here today. We need a DNA sample, you see, from a close family member. The body, unfortunately, has been dead for some time and the level of decomposition is such that visual identification is out of the question.

Kieran leaned back on the couch and looked over at his mother, who'd started whining again quietly.

'With that said, Mr Doyle - I'm sorry, I didn't catch your first name?'

'It's Kieran,' he said, turning back to look at Pommery. 'Mum told me it means 'little dark one'.'

Pommery raised his bushy eyebrows, curiously. 'Well, like I said, my name is Bill Pommery and I'm the Chief Inspector, based over in Neilston. So, regarding this matter of a DNA sample...' He pulled a small plastic baggie from his trouser pocket and handed it to Kieran. 'We need to take a small cheek swab - nothing more than that.'

Kieran looked down at the baggie in his hands. Inside was what appeared to be a cotton bud.

'If you wouldn't mind...' Pommery continued, motioning to the swab. 'It's clean, you can trust me. I just need a small sample. If you could insert the swab into your mouth and collect some of the skin cells from your cheek.'

Kieran's brow furrowed.

'It won't hurt I promise. I'm not trying to trick you.'

Kieran took the cotton bud from the baggy and placed it in his mouth like a lollipop.

Pommery looked satisfied. 'That's right, now just pop the swab back in the bag and hand it over to me.'

***

A few days later, Pommery arrived at the door of the Doyle's small bungalow once again. The news he brought this time would set the rest of Kieran's life into motion.

Chapter 18
Bankfoot

The car behind Claire beeped loudly, shaking her from her daze. Her pale blue Fiat 500 was waiting at the junction outside Neilston: left would take her back into town and most likely back to the hotel where she'd retire for the night, and right was the slip road that fed back onto the bypass, taking her east towards Glasgow. The car behind her beeped again and she saw him gesture at her in the mirror. She made up her mind... She slammed the car into first and spun the wheel right. She was getting herself the hell out of Dodge.

On the bypass back to Glasgow, she settled on her plan. There were four people left who were present that night in nineteen-ninety-seven: one of them was her, the other was her brother (currently en route back to Britain), one of them was in prison (whether guilty as charged or innocent, she had yet to decipher), and one of them lived in Bankfoot - or at least he had done the last time she'd visited.

Claire's uncle Jack had always been pleasant. He was the joker in the family and usually shouldered the burden of keeping the kids amused on shared holidays and family excursions. She'd liked him, and that helped her make up her mind - she would pay him a visit.

Jack's wife Molly had passed away several years ago. She received the news from her mother (another short and sweet text message). An overdose of medication, or so it had been billed. Whether she'd had the constitution for suicide, Claire had never known. She'd barely known the woman at all in her grownup years. Neither had she seen Jack since that Christmas in ninety-seven, so this visit would be somewhat unexpected. That was if they still lived at the same address of course. Jack could have moved in the years since his wife passed, but for some reason, and she couldn't fathom why, she was confident that he hadn't.

Bankfoot was a small village, eight miles outside of Perth, where the Hunt's had grown up. It would be a two-hour drive from Neilston, she estimated, but this gave her time to think about what she was going to say when she got there.

She doubted that Jack would recognise her; it had been ten years after all. She'd grown up a lot since she was in her teens, though her hair was almost the same and her figure hadn't changed. She just hoped he would be as welcoming and as friendly as he had been while she was growing up; although as a widower with a son recently put away for murder, she doubted it. Nevertheless, this was the last person who could give her the answers she so desired. One last person from the car that disappeared that night into the snowstorm.

***

As she reached the Broxden roundabout, on the western reaches of Perth, she took the turn North for Aberdeen. Bankfoot lay between Perth and the village of Dunkeld - the place where her parents had scattered her grandmother's ashes when she was just a little girl. This trip, however, would not be sentimental.

As she took the turn off for Bankfoot, the memory of her last visit hit her like a strike to the amygdala. She had been fourteen and it was winter - they always took turns visiting in the winter for the holidays. They played football in their garden while it snowed. Claire had been reaching that age where boys and girls subconsciously started splitting off into their own sexes and her interest in playing football in the garden with the boys had been waning. She remembered on that occasion though, it had been fun (slippy, but fun).

As she crossed into the village, she recognised the sign at the entrance.

'*Welcome to Bankfoot. Home of the MacBeth Experience*'

They'd visited it once as a family and had lunch at the visitor centre cafe. As for the play, she'd read it in high school and couldn't help but draw parallels between her mother and Lady Macbeth. As the countryside gradually turned into houses, she saw the hill in the distance that she knew the Hunt's house resided on.

Bankfoot was a village taken straight out of a bedtime story. It was a smattering of new houses and old farmhouses, centred around a hill upon which sat an old burnt down church. The skeletal remains of the church on the hill, and the old graveyard around it, gave the village a ghostly feel that was only increased by its apparent lack of occupants. As little as two hundred people lived in a village that once would've been a much more charming real estate investment. Once the new dual carriageway was built, that skirted the village, a good percentage of villagers had upped and left, in search of the peace and quiet that'd been stolen from them.

At the top of the hill behind the church sat the house she'd once known as a child. It was modest, compared to her own parents' residence, but still relatively attractive in a twee sort of way. The upkeep however, like her own childhood home, had taken a noticeable nosedive. The fence at the front of the garden had blown onto its side and the grass was longer than most of the skirts she had in her cupboard at home. It was a sorry sight to say the least, but despite this, she took hope from the fact there was a light on in the front room. Her uncle, perhaps? Or maybe it was some new owner who also had a knack for letting the housework get on top of them.

She parked on the street, two doors down from the house that she knew, so as not to alert anybody too early to her presence. The dark street was lit by two single streetlamps that provided enough light to cover only the houses in the middle. She turned the engine off and sat in her vehicle, thinking of the best way she could approach this. Eventually, she decided there was no better angle than old fashion dead on; she would tell her Uncle Jack, if it was him that was living there, that she was in the area and had decided to drop in for a visit. Despite it not really being plausible or believable, it was simple, and you couldn't argue with simple. She stashed the car keys in her bag and headed towards the house.

**

Arriving at the door, the porch light blinkered on, alerting whoever was in the front room to her presence. She knocked lightly and at the same time a face appeared in the window looking out at her. She heard movement behind the door then watched it creek open.

'Hello? Who's there?' said a voice through the gap.

Claire breathed a sigh of relief. She recognised his voice at once. 'Uncle Jack, it's me, Claire...'

'Claire? Claire Becker?' He unclipped the safety latch and swung the door open. Standing in the doorway was the shell of the man she'd once known. He looked withered by years of relentless alcohol abuse combined with general malnourishment. His skin was sallow and tight around his bones and his greying hair had all but fallen away, leaving a single tuft of grey that he'd swiped over to the side.

'Claire? Is that you?' he croaked. 'It's been years! Come in, won't you? I'll fix you a drink.'

Claire smiled widely and walked inside. The smell of smoke hit her immediately, almost making her wish she'd hadn't left her Nicolette inhaler in the car. The smell, however, wasn't the one of a freshly lit cigarette that she yearned for so badly; rather it was one of stale, wet, overflowing ashtrays that caught in her throat and made her want to vomit. All said, it wasn't the kind of house you'd want to wake up in on Christmas morning.

'Do you want me to take my shoes off?' she asked, doubting whether it would make much of a difference to the carpet.

'No, you're fine. Just come in,' he called over his shoulder from the living room.

The living room was lit by a single lamp perched on a table by the couch. Jack was standing by the fireplace where he'd set up a mini drinks station complete with crystal decanters and an ice bucket (not too dissimilar to her mother's).

'What's your poison?' he asked, as he scooped two large cubes of ice into a glass.

'Vodka please. If you have it.'

'Never did care much for the stuff. I might have some in the kitchen.' He took the glass and disappeared behind a door into the darkness.

'Yup. Thought so!' he called. 'I've an old bottle left over from years ago. Someone must have left it. That's the good thing about liquor - never goes out of date.' A minute later, he tottered back through to the living room holding a freshly filled glass of clear liquid.

'So, what can I do for you?' he asked, taking a sip from his own newly-topped-up glass.

Claire didn't know how to start. She hesitated and Jack filled the silence.

'I take it you heard about Adam?' he asked. 'What a right fucking mess - if you'll excuse my French.'

'I heard,' Claire said, taking a seat on the couch behind her. 'Have you seen him?'

'He came to see me the month before he went away. We hadn't spoken in years, then one day he arrived at the front door'

'How did he look?'

'Not great, if I'm honest. He said he'd been getting migraines, or something like that, and the doctors won't give him anything that works.'

'I'm sorry to hear that. I didn't realise you and Adam weren't speaking for so long...'

'Yeah... little prick cut me off after his mother died. Seemed to think I had something to do with that - although, I've no idea where he got that idea from. T'was as much a shock to me as it was to him. How was I supposed to know she was going to choke back a handful of those fucking pills she kept to help her sleep?'

Claire shifted in her chair uncomfortably and Jack let out a rasping, phlegm-filled cough.

'So, what brings you up this neck of the woods, if you don't mind me asking? Last I heard you were in London. Actually... I think I might've seen you on the news when all those terrorist attacks were going on.'

Claire smiled. 'I'm not in that line of work anymore. I teach at a primary school now.'

'In Scotland?'

'No, still in London. I actually came here tonight to share some quite troubling news with you... It's my mother...'

'Oh yeah. How's old Gwendolyn getting on these days?'

'Well, that's the thing. Not so good actually. She was found dead two days ago...'

Jack fell silent and stared at her for what seemed like the longest time. 'That's terrible...' he said at last. 'I'm very sorry to hear that. I always liked Gwen. She could be a bit unstable at times, no denying that, but I always felt deep down, she was one of the good ones, y'know?'

'Yeah, she was...' Claire lied. 'Actually, I did stop by for another reason as well... A question... One I had for my mother that she never got to answer. I was wondering if you could maybe help?'

'Sure. Ask away.'

'It's so long ago, I doubt you'll remember, but I wanted to ask you about a Christmas we spent together as a family a long time ago. I think it was nineteen-ninety-seven...'

Jack lowered his drink to the table and fixed her with a knowing glare. 'What do you know about that night?' he asked.

'Nothing. Absolutely nothing. It just occurred to me that my parents seemed to enter into a sort of downward spiral after that Christmas and I thought something maybe happened that might've caused that change?'

Jack snorted. 'Something happened all right.' He lifted his glass and threw back another drink. Claire could smell the whiskey from six feet away - he reeked of it.

'What happened, exactly?'

'Suppose there's no harm in telling you now. If what you say is true, then I guess I'm the last one still alive anyway and I don't give a fuck anymore.'

Claire gazed at him patiently, waiting for him to continue.

'It was all your dad's fault. That prick - sorry, but it's true...'

'What happened?'

'We went out in the car - the four of us. Left you kids at home. We were only going to be gone twenty minutes. Was meant to be a quick nip to the shop; pick up another case of beer and some wine for the ladies.'

'You didn't go to the off-licence?'

'No, we went all right. Loaded the boot full of booze. Then your dad wanted to have a little fun in the snow. A quick joyride in the country, then back before midnight. We were all so drunk we just went along with it. He was speeding and slamming on the brakes, making long skid marks in the snow. The roads were empty, you see, so we had the run of them.'

'Then what happened?' Claire prompted.

'Well, I'm not sure how it happened, but somehow we ended up all the way out near that big estate that was converted into a hotel some years back.'

'Montgreenan.'

'That's the one. You know it?'

'Driven past it a few times.'

'Well, Frank wanted to go in there, you see, as the roads are private and twisty. I think he thought he was Michael Cane in that movie – the one where he drives down those stairs. Must have been the drink. So, he made the turn off and drove into that estate and there was this other car coming towards us. We could see its headlights lighting up the snow - it was so beautiful.'

He coughed again loudly, taking a second to get his breath back. 'Frank slammed his foot down on the gas. I think he wanted to give the guy a fright. Your mother was egging him on in the front, and me and Molly were in the back - still laughing, but at the same time getting kind of worried. So, at the last moment he swings to the side and this guy must have got the fright of his life. He beeped his horn at us as he went past. Only, it wasn't a he... it was a she. As we drove past, we saw this young girl in the driver's seat, and she had a man with her in the passenger side.'

'She had somebody with her?!' Claire interrupted.

'Yeah. Older fella it looked like. Wait... how do you...?'

'Please, go on.' Claire encouraged him.

'So yeah, there was this girl driving the car and she must have taken Frank's fancy because he swung the car around and started following her. It looked like she got a fright because she started speeding up; trying to get away from him most likely. The roads were so slippery that night that we were both skidding all over the place. Then we saw her up ahead; she went into this corner too tightly, and she veered off the road and straight into a tree... Frank slammed on the brakes, but we just kept skidding. I was screaming from the back; *'turn! Fucking turn! You fucker!'* But it was no good... We went right into the back of her.'

Claire looked at him in disgust.

'Don't give me that look... It was your fucking father who was driving!'

Claire ignored him. 'Was she alive?'

'Yeah, she was fine. The car was just a little bashed up from where we'd hit it.'

'So, what happened then?'

'What do you mean? We got the fuck out of there as quickly as fucking possible, that's what happened.'

'But she died!' Claire cried, no longer able to contain herself. She was feeling strangely emotional all of a sudden.

Her uncle stared at her in surprise. 'How the fuck would you know that?'

'It was in the paper, that's how!' Claire fumed.

Her uncle stared at her disbelievingly. 'Yeah... she died. You're right, ok? She died!'

'Her name was Alice Doyle, and they found her at the bottom of a ravine seven months later.' She was almost brimming with rage now but remained in her seat.

'We didn't do that!' her uncle cried, rising from his seat and pacing towards the fireplace. 'There was movement in the car when we drove off. Both of them were fine. I have no idea how she ended up at the bottom of that ravine. None of us did... When we saw it in the paper, that they'd found her in a ravine, we were just as shocked as you...'

'You're telling me you're innocent?' Claire scolded.

'Innocent of killing her at least, if that's what you're accusing me of. Why don't you ask that guy who was in the car with her? Maybe he could tell you how she ended up down there.'

Claire had raised herself from the couch but stopped halfway through the motion. She felt dizzy.

She fell back against the pillow and stared up at her uncle, letting her eyes swim back into focus.

'You didn't kill her?' she whispered. 'Then who did?'

'That's what I'm telling you! We left her in the car. It was a shitty thing to do and I hate myself every day for doing it, but that's where we left it. We got home twenty minutes later and went to bed.'

'I remember,' Claire murmured. 'I was awake. I heard you all come in. You were arguing...'

'Yeah, because I wanted to go back to that estate and make sure they were alright. But Frank wouldn't have it... He kept saying it was best we cut and run, before the police got involved'.

Claire remembered hearing her own father's whispered voice on the porch steps that night. He'd seemed scared and anxious. Was it him that was to blame for all this? His idea to take the joyride and his idea to have some fun at Alice Doyle's expense?

'She was just a girl,' Claire muttered, starting to cry. 'How could you do this to her?'

'Maybe you should have asked your own father that question.' Jack was standing by the fire now looking longingly into the flames. 'Because I don't have an answer for you. You hear me? I don't have the fucking answer! Maybe Frank didn't either... Car accident, right? Supposedly an accident? But then again... he was pretty distraught...'

'My father didn't kill himself!' Claire spat at him.

'Neither did my wife. But who really knows for sure?'

'I knew my father. He wouldn't do that.'

141

'Clearly you didn't know him as well as you think.
I thought you would have realised that by now.'

Claire made to protest, then silenced herself.
Maybe she hadn't known her father as well as she had
thought...

Chapter 19
Evidence

Pommery was at a complete loss for words. He remembered ten years ago, visiting the Doyle's house with the intention of garnering some DNA from a family member. He remembered the state that the ramshackled property had been in - like something out of the television programme *'Life of Grime'*, that his wife used to watch, back when it was on the telly. The young boy that'd lived there then had looked nothing like the man who sat before him now. He could see no resemblance whatsoever.

'I met you once before...' Pommery said, breaking the silence that'd been building.

'That's right.'

'But you seem different now.' Pommery continued.

'Time will do that...'

'Indeed... So how is it that you're here? And let me ask you again: what were you doing with Miss Becker last night?'

'I was helping her...'

'Helping her with what?'

'Helping her to see how our families are invariably connected.'

'What do you mean?' Pommery asked, shifting in his chair.

'I think you know...'

'I most certainly do not.'

'Well in that case, let me do the police work for you.'

'Excuse me?' Pommery puffed.

'You were there on the day they found my sister's body, correct? Kieran asked.

'Yes... that's right.'

'Well in that case, you should be aware that her vehicle was found some months before, not far from where the body was discovered?'

'I am aware yes. We found her car out on the Montgreenan Estate, in January it was, I think. The licence plates had been stolen, so we had a hard time tracing the owner.'

'And did it not occur to you that the owner may have been an employee of the hotel?'

'That was the first thing that occurred to us,' Pommery said assuredly. 'We went up there that very day and talked to the manager - I can't remember his name, but it'll be on-file somewhere. He told us that to his knowledge, none of his employees owned the car in question.'

'And you believed him?' Kieran asked.

'What reason would we have not to? He seemed like a reasonable man. But this was all so long ago, I can hardly remember...'

'Strange... I remember it as if it were yesterday,' Kieran replied.

'Yes, well... that's understandable, seeing as...'

'She was my sister.'

'Right...'

'And how many arrests did you make after you'd found the body?'

Pommery shifted uncomfortably. 'Well, we didn't have any leads and the crime scene turned up nothing. There wasn't much to go on... No witnesses, no fingerprints, no DNA left by the body.'

'So, the killer got away then?' Kieran asked with a smirk - leading the Chief Inspector in a way he hadn't expected.

'There was no evidence to say that she'd even been murdered in the first place. For all we know, she could have fallen down that ravine completely of her own accord - while she was out walking in the woods, perhaps.'

Kieran looked angered. 'And the car? The missing plates? What about that? And the fact that nobody from the hotel reported that she hadn't turned up for work?'

'We did ask about that,' Pommery defended. 'We were told the hotel had a very high turnover of staff, and it wasn't uncommon for the younger ones to go AWOL and not even give so much as a phone call to inform the hotel that they were leaving.'

'That's bullshit!' Kieran scolded.

'Mr Doyle - if that's really who you are - I must ask again, what does all this have in connection with Miss Becker and her mother? We've had a murder happen right on our doorstep and you just so happened to be lurking at the scene of the damn crime!'

Kieran smiled, seeming to relax a little. 'I told you already - I was helping...'

'Helping with what, exactly?!' Pommery almost shouted, before collecting himself and resting his hands back on the table. 'Helping with what, may I ask?' he repeated, in a considerably cooler tone.

Kieran sighed deeply, as if collecting himself for the big reveal. Then he lay his clasped hands on the table beside Pommery's and began.

'Helping her to see what I've seen all these years. Helping her to recognise the truth about her family. About what they are – or were. About what they did...'

'You're not making any sense,' Pommery rebutted.

'Maybe not right now, but once you know what I know, you'll be able to see things the way I do.'

'And which way is that?'

Kieran sighed again and continued. 'On the night my sister was killed, multiple players were involved. Some of those players were members of Miss Becker's own family. She doesn't know it, but it was her father who crashed his bumper into the back of my sister's car. It was her parents who put in motion the chain of events that would lead to her death.'

'Excuse me?!' Pommery spat at him, nearly choking himself in the process. He breathed in a long raggedy breath then cleared his throat. 'Did you say Frank Becker? Frank Becker died in a car wreck six years ago. I attended the scene myself. He was well over the limit, lost control and flipped his car over an embankment.'

'I guess he felt he needed to pay for what he'd done...'

'Like I told you already, there's no evidence that Miss Doyle was killed by anyone... The scene was checked and checked again and each time it came up clean. Any potential suspect, if there ever was one, would've had to have been the most careful killer in the history of forensic investigation. Not one shed of DNA, other than her own, was found on that body. If there was a killer, he would have left something behind - like a hair or a fibre of clothing or skin cells.'

'I wouldn't know about that, but I do know beyond a shadow of a doubt that it was the Beckers' who crashed into her.'

'If what you're saying is true Mr Doyle, this not only puts you at the scene of the crime, but gives you motive as well. Motive for killing both Mr and Mrs Becker.'

'I didn't touch them.'

'Yes, well... we'll find that out shortly. Until then though, I don't think anyone would complain if we were to hold on to you for a few days - if only to make sure no more murders take place over the weekend.'

'Do what you like. It makes no difference.'

'Don't worry, we will,' Pommery said, rising to his feet. 'I'll have Officer Ward escort you to a holding cell. I'm going to call it a night. We'll talk more in the morning.' He left the room and locked the door behind him. 'Officer Ward, see that our guest has a good place to sleep tonight. I'm going down to evidence. Phone my wife and tell her I'll be late tonight, will you?'

'Right you are, Chief.'

Chapter 20
Natural Causes

Claire reached for her glass and took a much-needed drink of the icy clear liquid - she rarely drank vodka straight, but at that moment it didn't matter. She allowed herself another sip before lowering the glass onto the floor. Her uncle was still standing by the fire. 'Someone murdered my mother,' she gasped, struggling to accept the true meaning of the words she was saying. 'Who would do such a thing?'

Her uncle glanced over at her, then turned away quickly. 'Someone who knew the truth,' he said quietly into the flames. 'Your mother was just as guilty as your father. She egged him on, and I don't think he would have gone as far as he had if she hadn't approved of it. She was right there in the passenger seat, laughing and jeering.'

Claire felt tears well in her eyes. She didn't want to cry over her mother - the bitch had never been there for her since she'd grown up - but the fading memories of how she'd been when she was younger were all starting to flood back to her. She pictured her face,

young and inflectionless, a wide smile stretching ear to
ear as she cooked Claire's breakfast. Then she was sat
in a car, waving from the window and blowing her a
kiss, having just dropped her off at school. It was a
different woman to the one she knew now. A different
woman entirely.

'If what you're telling me is true, then Alice Doyle
was still alive when you left her...'

'She was. We saw she was. They were both
moving in the car - her and that fella she was with.'

'Who was he?'

'I've no idea. Some bloke. Maybe he worked at the
hotel and she was giving him a lift home?'

Claire considered this for a moment before
speaking. 'If that's true, then this man is likely the last
person to see her alive. Maybe even the person
responsible for what happened to her. We've got to
find out who he was...'

'You're kidding me, right? That was ten years ago.
Everyone's moved on. It's forgotten.'

'Someone clearly hasn't forgotten. My mother's
dead remember, and it certainly wasn't of *natural
causes*.' She flashed on her mother's splayed body once
more, then squeezed her eyes shut to clear the image.
'Someone is out there who knows the truth, and
someone has a score to settle. My mother's murder is
proof of that.'

'Maybe you're right... Maybe there is someone out
there.'

Claire checked her watch - five minutes to
midnight. she was hit by a wave of tiredness that she

hadn't felt coming. 'It's late. I better get going. I'm sorry to have disturbed you so late.'

'No problem at all. I rarely sleep these days anyway. Stop by anytime.'

Claire rose from the couch and the glass by her feet spilled over onto its side. 'Shit! I'm sorry.' The clear liquid spilled out, leaving a small round stain on the carpet.

'Don't worry about it. Here, let me show you out.' He led Claire to the door and opened the clasp for her. 'Oh, one more thing, before you go...

Chapter 21
Tucked Away

Bill Pommery flicked the switch at the top of the long flight of stairs that led down to the basement. The basement at the Neilston police station served nicely as both the evidence room and the break room. Since the lights were switched off just now, however, he could safely assume that no one was down there on their break.

At the bottom of the stairs, he flipped another switch and the basement came to life. Shelves upon shelves stacked with boxes marked with dates and serial numbers, some going all the way back to the fifties. In fact, the oldest case they had on file here was an unsolved murder from nineteen-fifty-seven, involving a young girl, not unlike Alice Doyle.

He made his way towards the back, which was the darkest corner of the room and contained some of the older boxes that had been gathering dust for generations. It was procedure in Scotland to incinerate all evidence after an eighteen-year period; however, Pommery knew for a fact that this practice was rarely followed to the letter (and at his own station, it seemed, it wasn't followed at all).

He found the row with a small paper card marking the year '1998' in faded black marker. He saw the box he was looking for and heaved it down to the floor. A little plume of dust filled the air as he did so, causing him to fight off a small coughing fit as he lowered himself to his knees (he would have squat if he could've managed it, but his bad knee would no longer allow for that kind of pliable movement). The top of the box had the standard procedural form sellotaped to its cover. '*98: A-D*', read the top left-hand corner. Bill laughed silently to himself thinking, 'this is an old box for sure, but not quite ninety-eight years after Christ old'.

He unstuck the sellotape from the sides and pried the lid open. Inside were a few polyurethane bags filled with decaying samples of evidence and a small pile of folders. He pulled the folders out and scanned them for one marked 'Doyle'. It didn't take long to find what he was looking for. The folder in question was one of the lightest (highly unusual for a murder case).

Bill removed the two elastic bands that held it together and lay it flat on the ground. He flicked through the pages and found what he was looking for. *Fingerprint Samples*. There was another poly bag attached to the document showing three clear prints that had been lifted from the scene. Bill held it to his face and examined the notes next to each of them.

The first fingerprint was taken from the steering wheel of the car found in the Montgreenan Estate and had been matched to Alice Doyle. The second one was taken from the door handle of the driver-side of the vehicle and also belonged to Miss Doyle. The third print, however, taken from the door handle of the passenger-side of the vehicle, was marked as unknown. The text next to the print read: *'Print from unknown sub. Possibly related to victim as whirl pattern of print is close, but not a direct match.'*

Pommery frowned. He couldn't remember writing this down, but the handwriting was clearly his own. He felt immediately frustrated that he hadn't done more to track the owner of this third print at the time it was collected. Suddenly, an idea occurred to him. Hadn't they just taken prints from Kieran Doyle when they'd booked him upstairs a few hours ago?

He grabbed the open file, stashed it beneath his arm and headed for the stairs. Back in the station, he saw Officer Ward lounging at his desk.

'Don't worry, Chief, I've tucked him away for the night,' he said, seeing Pommery emerge from the stairway.

'Have you uploaded his prints yet?'

'Just doing that now.'

Pommery pulled a chair and spun it around to the young officer's desk. 'Let me see,' he said, taking the print sheet from his hands.

'I've just scanned them, Chief. They're up on the DB.'

Pommery ignored him. He lay the folder on the desk and held the newly taken print next to the unknown one taken from the vehicle.

'Can I ask what you're looking for?' Ward said, peering over his shoulder.

'I want to see if these new prints from our guest, match up with these old ones.' He grabbed the magnifying glass from the young officer's stationary cup that was filled with pencils and covered in St Mirren badges, and held it to his eye. Slowly, he went over both prints, checking for similarities.

'They match?' Ward asked.

Pommery slumped. 'No. Not quite. But they're similar.' He pointed to the first print. 'See how the whirl in the centre matches this one? They're almost identical except for friction ridges here that're different.'

'What are you trying to prove, exactly?' Ward asked.

'I was curious whether our new guest was involved in an old unsolved murder case I worked on ten years ago.'

'Who? Mr Grey?'

'Actually. He prefers the name Mr Doyle. We were right, he isn't the Grey's long-lost son after all. Turns out that Mr Doyle has some old unresolved beef with an unsolved murder case. That of his sister, if you can believe that...'

'Shit...' Ward clasped his hands behind his head and gawked at him. 'Don't tell me you think he killed the Becker woman?'

Pommery frowned. 'I don't know. When we get the samples back from the lab, we'll know for sure. But until then, I think it's safe to assume he's innocent, of that crime at least.'

'You sure? Seems like a good fit?'

Little Dark One

'He doesn't strike me as killer. Don't get me wrong, the guy is creepy as hell, but not the cold-blooded killer kind of creepy, unfortunately.'

'You think he had something to do with it?'

'Maybe. We'll find out soon. Get these prints filed away for me, will you? I want you and Officer Nicol to take a trip for me.'

'Sure thing, Chief. Where we going?'

'The Montgreenan hotel. I think it's time we paid the manager another visit...'

Ward checked his watch and looked out at the rain. 'It's past midnight. Can it wait until morning?'

Pommery hadn't realised the time. 'Shit, I better get home - Mandy's gonna kill me.'

Ward laughed as the Chief dropped everything, grabbed his jacket and ran for the door. 'G'night Chief!'

Chapter 22
Croissants and Cappuccinos

The next morning, officers Luke Ward and Ryan Nicol were sat in the patrol car headed towards Irvine. Nicol was the one driving, as usual, and Ward sat in the front seat and adjusted the radio stations - switching between music and chat radio - keeping the volume low so they could still hear the dispatch. Ward turned it to the football scores and Nicol blurted, 'Hey! I was listening to that!'

'Your bad taste in music is one of the reasons I'm getting out of this racket.' Ward had long been planning to hand his resignation in to Pommery but wanted to wait until the timing was just right. His young wife, Flora, owned a little delicatessen in the town centre called 'Flora's' and he was planning to help her run it full-time (as opposed to the occasional afternoons he could manage at the moment).

'Still planning on abandoning us, then?' Nicol asked.

'Two months from now it'll be freshly baked sourdough, croissants and cappuccinos - what more can a man ask for?'

'You'll get sick of it, believe me. You'll come crawling back to Pommery in a year from now, begging him to take you back.'

'I don't think so, amigo. This is my destiny.'

'Sour dough is your destiny?'

'That's right. So is getting to spend time with my wife. D'you know how long it's been since we actually got to spend a whole weekend together?'

'Weekends? What are those?'

'Exactly. You should think about tendering *your* resignation as well. We've got space for you in the kitchen. You can wash the dishes.'

'Fuck you. I'll pass. Another two years and I'll make Sergeant.'

'You think so?'

'I do.'

'Well, I wouldn't hold your breath - shit! That's the turnoff!' Ward pointed to the large stone archway at the entrance to the Montgreenan Estate and Nicol swerved the car sharply - just making the exit with inches to spare.

'Haven't been here in years,' Nicol remarked, as he took the first speed bump at the designated five miles per hour.

'Looks nice...' Ward offered, taking in the grounds. 'Someone's been working hard to keep this place looking in top shape. Just look at those hedges... trimmed to perfection.'

'Reminds me of that scene from the Shinning. Y'know with the hedge animals?'

'Is that in the book or the movie?' Ward asked.

'The book of course. Wasn't a fan of the movie.'

'How come?'

'Just wasn't as good.'

'Well, they rarely are.' Ward replied.

The car started shaking as Nicol drove onto the pebbles in front of the hotel. 'What did the Chief say again? Be subtle but forceful?'

'Yeah, something like that. Come on - I'll do the talking.' Ward pushed his door open and stretched his legs in the fresh air. 'Can you believe it? It's not raining for once.'

'Maybe it's going to be a good day after all.'

The two young officers made their way up the steps towards the grand doorway at the entrance. The inside of the hotel was plush with crimson red carpets. There were enormous framed paintings lining the walls like some sort of art gallery. They all depicted aspects of the vast Scottish countryside, and Ward recognised the Glenfinnan viaduct from the *Harry Potter* films in the painting nearest to them.

There were two young ladies manning the reception. One was on the phone and the other favoured them with a welcoming smile. 'What can I do for you two gentlemen?'

'A word with the manager please, if you wouldn't mind, love?'

'Of course. I'll just see if he's available.' She picked up her phone and placed a quick call. Ward and Nicol shuffled awkwardly on the spot until she was done.

'He'll be down in just a moment. He's currently holding a small briefing for staff in the conference room. If you'd like to take a seat while you wait?' She pointed to three tartan-upholstered chesterfield armchairs behind them.

'No thanks, we'll stand,' Officer Nicol replied.

Five minutes later, a man made his way down the staircase in front of them. He was short, perhaps sixty-years old, and extremely well presented. His hair was slicked into a parting with pinpoint precision.

'Gentleman. I am so sorry to keep you waiting. My name is Lawrence Kelso - general manager of the Montgreenan Hotel. How may I help you?' he said, shaking each of their hands on arrival.

'Is there somewhere we can talk privately?' asked Officer Ward.

'Of course! The cigar room should be sufficient. Of course, these days it's less of a cigar room and more of a general smoking room. You don't get many who still appreciate the exquisite texture of a finely rolled cigar. Of course, I don't partake myself, but I've always been tempted by the beautiful aroma they produce - this way please.' He led the two young officers along the hallway, past the bar and what looked like the restaurant and through to a small chamber that resembled a bank vault.

The room was dark with heavy curtains drawn over the windows. The dim lighting from little kerosene lamps gave it an eerie candlelit effect. As they entered, Ward saw the bookshelves full of dusty old volumes that nestled against the walls. The room reminded him of an evil villain's lair, or the first-class lounges on the Titanic - which, he couldn't decide.

'This room was once the personal vault of his Lordship the Viscount Weir. I can only image the sorts of treasures that were locked inside. And there's the man himself...' He pointed to a life-sized portrait of the Viscount Weir hanging on the wall beside a large bookshelf. He was an elderly gentleman, wearing full hunting regalia. One arm was rested on a rifle he was using to hold himself up. The two officers nodded at the painting appreciatively.

'Now what seems to be the matter?' Mr Kelso asked, as he took his seat in one of three antique armchairs collected around a table in the deepest corner of the room.

Ward sat opposite him and extracted his notepad and pencil from the inside pocket of his utility vest. 'We appreciate your time, Mr Kelso,' he began. 'The matter is actually one that took place on the grounds of this estate quite some time ago. A young girl was found in the woods - perhaps you remember?'

Me Kelso frowned, as if deep in concentration. 'Yes, I think I do remember that. The poor thing fell down an embankment?'

'That's the one,' Ward replied. 'I realise this might be asking a lot given the time that's passed, but if you could stretch your memory that far, we'd like to ask you some questions?'

'It was a very long time ago,' Kelso mused. 'But I will do my best, of course.'

'Thank you. Now, how long have you been in your position at the Montgreenan hotel?'

'Fifteen years. Since the house was originally converted to a hotel. I knew the Viscount personally and it's been an honour to keep his beloved home in such tip-top condition.'

'And do you remember the incident in question?'

'Yes, I remember now. How could I not? Such a tragedy, poor young thing. And to learn she worked at this very hotel... So tragic. I didn't know her socially, of course, but I remember her face. We have a very high turnover of staff at the Montgreenan, and most only stay for a matter of months before they move on.'

'And why do you think that is?'

'Why? I couldn't possibly fathom. If you're suggesting that working conditions are anything less than exemplary then I assure you, you're mistaken...'

'No, of course... That's not what I meant,' Ward backtracked quickly. 'I'm sure it's a very nice place to work.'

'That, it most certainly is,' Kelso hmphed.

'Can you remember anything out of the ordinary happening around that time?'

'Oh, it was so long ago now... I spoke to the police at the time and told them everything I knew.'

'I realise that Mr Kelso, but if you could try your hardest... Was there anything at all that stuck out as peculiar?'

'Well - as I told the police at the time - I can remember her leaving with a man I hadn't seen before. He looked much older than her. I presumed she had a taste for older men - some of the younger girls are like that. Only after money you see... Anyhow, I can remember thinking it was strange as I'd never seen her with this man before.'

'What did he look like?' Ward asked, scribbling in his notepad.

'Definitely older. Perhaps in his late forties, or early fifties.'

Ward flashed back to what the Chief had said about the prints they'd taken from the passenger-side of the car, *so similar that they could be related.* 'Do you think the man could have been her father?' he asked.

Mr Kelso considered this. 'Perhaps... although that didn't strike me at the time. He seemed unfamiliar to her; as if they were still getting acquainted. Not the kind of dynamic one expects to see between a father and his daughter.'

Ward wrote this down in his notebook. 'Is there anything you can remember about the man's appearance? Hair colour for instance?'

'Forgive me, it was so long ago that I barely remember seeing the man at all... he's nothing but a blur to me now... I don't know, Brown hair perhaps? I can't be sure.'

'That's ok. We appreciate you trying anyway.'

'Like I said, I told all of this to the police at the time, so you should already have this information.'

Ward ignored him but couldn't help admitting that he had a point. 'For my benefit then; is there anything else you remember?'

'Yes. I remember she had an odd expression as she was leaving. She was always quite a timid girl, but on that day, it was almost like she looked frightened...'

'Frightened?'

'Yes - as she was leaving, I would have to say she almost looked scared... I could have misinterpreted it of course, but that's how she seemed to me.'

'And you remember this vividly, despite it being so long ago?'

'Yes, very vividly. She seemed frightened.'

'Ok, thank you, Mr Kelso,'

'Please. Call me Lawrence.'

'Thank you, Lawrence. I think that's as much of your time as we're going to need just now. You've been a great help.'

'My pleasure. If there's anything else you need, don't hesitate to stop by.'

'We won't...'

Chapter 23
Freckles

Claire sat in the car outside her uncle's house and
stared at the streetlights. The buttery hue of yellow lit
the inside of the car and made the skin on her arm look
jaundiced and sallow. She stared at her arm and saw
the freckles that she'd inherited from her mother. She
wondered just what else she had inherited from her.
Would she turn out the same? A drunken recluse sat
by the fireplace in a big empty house. Gradually
working her way through a bottle of vodka that she'd
spilled onto the floor at her feet. She wondered if it
were true that all women eventually turned into their
mothers. From the evidence so far, she didn't like the
road she was taking - she knew where it led to. Where
it ended. Was this where she was going? Her destiny?
She hated to think so.

All that was left for her to do now was turn the car
around at the end of the cul de sac and head off west
again to Neilston. The funeral still needed arranging
and there were other familial obligations that she'd
been putting on hold - like informing what was left of

her relatives. As the eldest surviving member of the dwindling Becker tribe, she was now the one responsible for such tasks. What a nightmare.

She started the engine and slid the car into first. Her responsibilities could wait, at least a little while longer - no one would blame her. Who was even left to blame her? No one. That's right. The drive north to Deepwood would take the better part of three hours, through the night, but she had all but given up on getting any sleep this evening anyway.

Chapter 24
Pieces of the Puzzle

Kieran Doyle sat in the small holding cell alone and stared through the bars. He didn't mind the solitude. He was used to it. He'd been alone most of his life; well, at least since his mother died. After Alice had left them, Kieran had tended to their mother as best as he could. The logical thing would have been to bring in a carer to look after her, but that would have required picking up the phone - something he'd only recently found the strength within him to accomplish. He knew why the thought of picking up the phone had always terrified him so acutely; he was scared that one day the phone would ring, and he'd pick it up and they'd tell him that Alice was never coming back. If he never picked up the phone, then that day would never happen. Of course, the arrival of Chief Inspector Pommery at his door had changed that for good. After that, the fear, now irrelevant, had remained - for what reason, he didn't know.

When his mother had died, four years, six months and twenty-two days ago, he'd moved out of the house that he'd lived in all his life. He'd travelled for a bit, before settling back down in Neilston. With the money his mother had left him in her will, he bought the car that now sat in the driveway of the Grey farm. He'd lived in that house for nearly seven years now. It was sheer luck that he'd stumbled across it - empty, abandoned and screaming to be occupied. He didn't need the whole house, just the extension had suited him fine. If the lights had started to flicker on and off in the main house, then it surely would've started to attract unwanted attention from the people in town.

Luckily, the extension to the old farmhouse was tucked neatly out of sight, away from prying eyes. He rarely had any of the lights on anyway - he preferred to read by daylight. And when it got too dark to read the page of a newspaper, he would use his torch that he'd found in the tool shed. The Grey's had left a lot of useful items behind when they'd died. He'd even started to warm to the pictures of them on the walls; starting to think of them as sort of a second family, or the father he'd never known. In his mind they were always there for him, smiling and staring at him lovingly. He knew their names from the collection of mail that'd amassed beneath the front door, but he preferred to just call them mum and dad, and they called him son.

He'd found life at the farm surprisingly easy. He made few trips into town (only for food supplies and essentials) and he'd been just polite and noncommittal enough to glide effortlessly under the radar - merely an afterthought as opposed to a question mark that would garner interest.

His research into the death of his sister had slowly become his life's work, and now, with everything that was happening, he sensed that it was quickly approaching completion. He'd discovered that the owners of the unknown car involved in the collision with his sister had been the Becker's some years ago. It was the initial reason he came to this neck of the woods in the first place - to observe them. The fact that there'd been a place for him to stay, hassle free, while he did so, had been an exceptionally fortunate coincidence.

When he looked at the house now it was just Mrs Becker, alone and drinking herself into an early grave. He sometimes saw her in the garden, stumbling and staggering like some wino you'd come across in the park. His hatred towards the Beckers', once absolute, had waned in recent years, after the father had met his own untimely end, somewhat justly, at the wheel of his burnt-out red Mondeo.

Claire, it seemed, was the final piece in the puzzle. The last chapter before completion. The arrival of the Becker's daughter had been somewhat unexpected, but he sensed that she had some part to play in all of this. After all, it was her family too - and her family were dead, just like his own.

Sitting now in his holding cell at the Neilston police station, he felt a peacefulness steal over him - the way a man who's built a house from the ground up must feel when there's only the front door left to paint before its completion. One last piece and the puzzle would be complete.

Chapter 25
Punch and Judy

Claire had no qualms about breaking the speed limit as she hurtled down the backroads. The car she'd rented wasn't exactly the fastest, but with her foot to the floor, pedal to the metal, she was pushing eighty and taking the bends at speeds that would've made the hearts of even the most daring of rally drivers skip the odd beat or two.

At this rate she would make it to Deepwood by daybreak or perhaps even sooner. Truth be told, visiting hours wouldn't begin until at least nine o'clock, so there really was no need for this urgency, but she found she couldn't help herself. The freeing feeling of throwing caution to the wind and letting instinct consume her, had, for the first time in days, allowed her to forget all about the harrowing mess she was in.

The faster she drove the lighter her chest felt. The weightlessness grew within her into an all-encompassing exhilaration, until she couldn't contain it anymore - she screamed into the steering wheel - feelings of pain and anger melding into one irrepressible cry of release. *She was free of her mother!* Despite the gruesome way in which she'd met her end, she was finally free.

She closed her eyes and tears started welling behind her lids, and before she could help it, they were streaming down her cheeks. She laughed as the first drops breached onto her lips; tasting the salty moisture on her tongue. As she raised her hand to wipe the tears away, she felt a wave of dizziness overcome her.

Suddenly, a car careened passed her in the act of overtaking. The man slammed on his horn as he passed her – she had unknowingly drifted out onto the far side of the road. Her head had started to swim again, and she was struggling to focus. As she turned the wheel slightly to merge back onto her own side, she felt her mind drift into total unconsciousness.

When she came to, she panicked and overcompensated on the wheel in the other direction. She corrected first to the right, then to the left, but the initial turn had been much too zealous. As her car swerved dangerously onto the opposite side of the road, she hit the brakes and tried to turn back again, but it was too late - the nose of the car was now facing back the way she'd come.

As the wheels hit the edges of the embankment, the car flipped into the air like a skateboard. Claire was thrown against the window, which smashed as the car bounced onto its bonnet. As it began its second turn, it smacked solidly into a tree; crunching the hood inwards and smashing any remaining glass that was left un-shattered.

The impact sent Claire's organs thrashing against her torso - her spleen quickly rupturing under the catastrophic pressure beneath her ribcage. The airbag compressed against her chest, holding her in place like a limp Punch and Judy puppet, legs and arms suspended over branches intruding through the windshield. Skirting on the edges of consciousness and bleeding out through the tear in her celiac artery, Claire began slipping into haemorrhagic shock. She opened her eyes and could see the blood on the airbag. Then she opened her mouth and took the last breath she would ever take.

Chapter 26
The Subtle Art of Delivering Bad News

When Pommery got back the next morning, he'd only just sat down at his desk when the call came in from the Pitlochry police station. There'd been an accident on the road between Grantully and Aberfeldy. One female passenger, dead on arrival. Pommery balked when he received the name.

'Are you sure?' he asked, frantically.

'Pretty sure. She had her driving licence in her handbag. Two registered addresses: one in London and one in Neilston. Thought I'd give you a phone first since your local. It's not pretty - believe me. Looks like she skidded first then flipped the car into some trees. Could have been a deer - who knows? They're pretty common on those roads and this is certainly the time of year for them. Anyway, we've sent the body over to Perth Royal Infirmary for safe keeping. The morgue should claim her soon. Then I guess her family will want her back in Neilston. I'm assuming her parents live nearby?'

Pommery closed his eyes and felt his throat spasm as he tried to swallow. 'Actually, her mother just died, not two days ago...'

'You're kidding?' Came the reply from the other end.

'Afraid not. Homicide, it looks like. It's an active case and we've just detained our first suspect.'

'Holy shit. Forgive my French, but that is all kinds of fucked up. Are there any others?'

'Father died some years ago and there's the youngest son, I think, who's deployed somewhere with the army. 'S'pose I'll have to get in touch with him somehow. Will try giving the barracks over in Prestwick a call and go from there.'

'Poor guy... lost his mother and his sister in the same week... what are the odds of that?'

'A million to one...'

'Anyway, sorry to have to be the bearer of bad news. Those backroads are a killer. This is the fifth fatality this year and that's in Perth and Kinross alone. I hope the rest of your day gets better.'

'Thanks. You too.' Pommery hung up the phone and sat with his hands behind his head. What a nightmare this week was quickly turning into. Two deaths in the space of a few days. He hadn't seen that in the whole of his thirty-five years on the force. What the hell would he tell the brother? It was shameful, but he was clutching at the vain hope that he could pass the news on to one of the young lad's commanding officers who would then dish the dirty. How do you tell a man he's lost his mother and his sister in the space of a week? He couldn't imagine possibly having

174

to deliver worse news, and he'd done his fair share of grief management during his time. They sent him on courses for it back in the early days; 'how best to deliver bad news in times of *stress*'. What expressions to wear, what body language to use, what words to avoid; there were entire books written on the subtle art of delivering bad news. In his experience, however, there was only one way to go, and that was straight down the middle. No faff or needless pandering; just say what you came to say and then get the hell out of there. Like ripping off a plaster - quick and painful. Still... he was hoping he wouldn't be the one who had to do it.

Just as he was about to reach for the phone again, to place the call to the Prestwick barracks, his phone rang for a second time. He picked it up. 'Bill Pommery,' he said warily.

'Chief, it's Luke,' came the voice of Officer Ward from the other end. 'We've just dropped in on the Montgreenan place as requested. We managed to get some time with Lawrence Kelso, the manager...'

'And...?'

'And he was reluctant to put his name to any details from so long ago, but he did mention one thing that I think you might be interested in.'

'What was it?' Pommery urged.

'Well, the fingerprints from the unsub in the passenger seat; you mentioned that they were similar to the ones from the Doyle girl, but not an exact match. The sort of similar that might be found on a member of the same family - a father, for instance.'

'Yes, that's right.'

'Well, Mr Kelso mentioned that he remembered seeing Miss Doyle leaving the hotel that night with an older man. I asked him if he thought the man could've been her father and he said it was possible.'

Pommery considered this for a moment. The idea had occurred to him of course - last night when he was on the floor of the evidence room with the fingerprint samples. Strangely though, it hadn't occurred to him ten years ago, during the original investigation. Had his mind been so distracted by other leads that he'd missed this one entirely? Or had he been lazy and complacent and overlooked what'd been staring him in the face? He guessed, either way, it was too late to change anything now. But then again, he had visited the Doyle's house over in Barrhead at the time and there'd been no father present then. The boy had told him himself, if was just him, his sister and their mother (who was heavily disabled). It was possible the father had recently left the picture, but he didn't think it likely. The way the boy had said it was as if there'd never been a father to begin with. Obviously, there must have been at some point, but not one that he'd known. It was possible that he was out of the picture immediately after he was born, or not long thereafter.

'Good work. Listen, I've just had some troubling news.'

'What is it Chief?'

'Miss Becker was killed in a car accident last night, up north near Aberfeldy.'

'The daughter? Are you serious?'

'Deadly serious, I'm afraid.'

'Bloody hell. What are the odds of that?'

'A million to one...' Pommery repeated.

'What a week...'

'It sure is.' He hung up the phone and spun out of his chair. It was time for him to have another little discussion with Mr Doyle. Perhaps there was more to his family tree than meets the eye.

Chapter 27
The Carpenter

Kieran was asleep in his cell when Pommery arrived in the holding room. There were three holding cells situated at Neilston Police Station. Most weekends they had to look after the local drunk or the occasional husband or boyfriend accused of domestic violence. It wasn't always the men either. He'd locked away plenty of women in his time for the same crime.

Tonight however, only Cell 1 had an occupant and that was Mr Doyle. Pommery wrapped his nightstick against the bars. 'Wakey, wakey, Mr Doyle.'

The man beneath the sheet began to stir and rolled over to face him.

'Would you like the continental or the full English this morning? I trust your stay has been comfortable?'

Kieran groaned and rubbed his eyes with the heel of his hand. 'What do you want?' he managed eventually.

'I'm afraid I bring bad news... Your friend, Claire Becker, was involved in a car accident up north.

Unfortunately, she didn't make it… She passed away before the emergency services arrived at the scene.'

Kieran sat bolt upright in his bunk and stared at him. 'She's dead…?' he asked, tentatively.

'I'm afraid so. It looks like she may have been speeding and lost control. I received a call from the Pitlochry Police Station this morning, informing me of the news.'

Kieran's head dropped and he stared at his lap.

'On another note, I'd like to ask you a few more questions, if you would oblige me?'

'When can I get out of here?'

'That all depends on whether we decide to charge you, Mr Doyle. As it stands, we can hold you for another thirty-six hours before making that decision.'

'I didn't kill anyone…' he said, defensively.

'In that case you won't have anything to worry about then, but for right now, sit tight and do what we ask of you.'

'Fine. What did you want to ask me?'

'You're father… I understand he wasn't in the picture?'

'I don't have a father.'

'In that case, I'm assuming, he left before you were born?'

Kieran shrugged, but Pommery took that as an affirmative. 'It's possible your sister had a relationship with your father that you never witnessed. I understand she was quite a bit older than you?'

'Eight years older. Where are you going with this?'

Little Dark One

'We spoke to the manager at the Montgreenan Hotel and he shared with us some information that may implicate your father.'

'I told you, I don't have a father.'

Pommery ignored him. 'We have three sets of fingerprints, all very similar. Two of them belong to you and your sister, but the third is, as yet, unidentified.'

This seemed to peak Kieran's interest. 'Where were the third set of prints found?'

'On the passenger-side door of your sister's vehicle.'

'The man she was with?'

'Correct. So, I'll ask you again. Did you know your father?'

Kieran shook his head, disjointedly.

'Do you at least know his name?'

'I never asked. He didn't exist to me. What good would a name do me?'

'Is there anything you know about him? Anything at all that could help us?'

'A picture...'

'Picture? What picture?'

'My sister kept a picture in her purse. I saw it once while she was paying at the supermarket. I think that was him...'

'Do you remember what he looked like?' Pommery urged.

'No, not really. But I think I have it at the house. I kept a few of her things with me after I moved away.'

'At the Grey's farmhouse on Riker's Road?'

180

'Yes, in the new building at the back. That's where I kept all my stuff.'

Pommery headed back towards the office immediately. He would contact Officer Ward and Nicol and tell them what he needed.

***

'Righto, Chief. We're on it,' Ward barked into his shoulder walkie. They were on their way back from Montgreenan, having stopped for some coffee in Lugton; Officer Nicol was driving, and Officer Ward tuned the station on the car's radio back to the music he'd been enjoying.

'What did he want?' Nicol asked.

'Wants us to drop in on the Grey's farm again. Apparently, there's a photograph in an old purse lying around the house somewhere.'

'Did he say who the photograph was of?'

'No, but I'm guessing that it's likely Mr Doyle Senior - our mystery gentleman caller.'

'Daddy not-so-cool?'

'Exactly. I still can't believe it about that Becker girl... What a waste.'

'How old was she?'

'Can't have been that much older than me. Late twenties I'm guessing.'

'Have they told the brother yet?'

'Not sure. Chief said he'd phone the barracks down in Prestwick.'

'Poor bastard. Not the news you want to get when you're off in some shithole fighting sand monkeys.'

'Not the news you want to get anywhere...'

Nicol turned the ageing BMW estate car onto the dirt road. 'I hate driving up this thing.'

'Look on the bright side. Maybe you'll fuck up the suspension and they'll have to give us a new one.'

'Or a shitty Astra. I'd rather keep hold of this, thank you very much.' He turned the car at the crossroad and trudged the short distance over the potholes to the Grey farm, stopping on the bank of weeds that skirted the driveway.

'Looks empty.'

'Of course, it's empty.'

'Do we knock? Doubt it's open. Might need to break a window.'

'Well, you can do the honours. This shirt's just been washed.'

'Is it my problem you only wash your shirts once a week?'

'It is now,' Nicol replied.

The two officers exited the squad car and circled around the main house, past the barn and the busted old tractor and to the newer building where Mr Doyle had been squatting, unbeknownst to the small community of Neilston. Ward grabbed a large rock from the back garden and smashed it through one of the panelled windows of the door.

'You might've tried the handle first...' Nicol said, amused.

Ward stuck his arm through the broken glass and felt around for a lock with his hand. 'No good. Looks like we'll need a key. Should I break one of the bigger windows?'

'Chief might have our balls if he finds out.'

'Fuck it.' Ward picked up the rock again and hurtled it through the glass window of the old farmhouse.

'Nicely done - idiot.'

'Well, we're in, aren't we?' He used his foot to kick out the long prongs of glass that remained attached to the window frame. 'After you.'

Nicol rolled his eyes and ducked through the opening, using his hands on the window frame to balance himself.

Inside was dark and more than a little dusty.

'Man, what a shithole,' Nicol said, dusting himself off.

'Like you could afford a place like this...' Ward replied, making his own way through the window.

'You know what I mean. It's big but it could do with a good clean. Look at the amount of dust on my trousers from that window! Nobody's cleaned this place in years.'

'Well, it was technically abandoned...'

'I can't decide whether this Doyle guy is a genius or a psychopath.'

'Probably a bit of both. Give me a hand, will you?'

Nicol reached out a hand to help Ward - whose leg had snagged on a splintered piece of wood - through the window. Once the two men were successfully through the gap, Nicol tried the light switch. 'No lights. Looks like the electricity is shut off.'

'Doubt there's hot water either - how has that filthy bastard been washing himself?'

'Cold showers?'

'His dick must be the size of a cashew by now...'

'Like yours, you mean?'

'Fuck you. You know I'm packing a monster in my pants; you've seen it.'

'Yeah, and I wish I hadn't...' Nicol shuddered at the memory.

'Looks like we'll need torches.' Ward unclipped the small torch that was fastened to his belt and shone it around the room. 'This place gives me the creeps...'

'You can say that again.'

The two men made their way slowly through the lower landing of the farmhouse. Trying the lights in each room and finding each of them lifeless. As they entered into the dining room, they stood staring in bewilderment.

'What the fuck is that?'

'Looks like newspapers,' Nicol replied.

'Who the fuck keeps so many papers?'

Against the back wall were dozens of piles of newspapers, stacked over six feet high.

'Maybe he reads the cartoons?' Ward asked.

'No, that's you that does that.'

'Oh yeah.'

They left the dining room and found the bathroom beside it.

'I'm going to be sick,' Ward said, covering his mouth with his free hand. The bathtub had turned green and was growing what appeared to be the latest discovery of penicillin.

'I wouldn't look in the toilet if I were you,' Nicol said, cringing away from the toilet bowl.

'Don't worry I won't.'

Ward led them upstairs, using his torch to guide the way. He used his elbow to push open the bedroom door to his left. Inside was something unlike anything they'd ever seen before.

Beside the bed, with an almost glowing emanation lighting the room, was what they would later describe as *'one of the most twisted shrines imaginable'*. It featured a cabinet with a large picture of Alice Doyle propped on the middle shelf. Around it were candles burned so low the wax had dripped and dried in long teardrops down the wood. Around the picture sat an assortment of bizarre items Officer Ward assumed belonged to the man's sister (although he hoped some of them didn't). There was a hairbrush - the hair had been removed from it and made it to a bizarre little 'hair doll' that was propped against the picture. There was a scattering of loose tampons; a tube of lipstick; some underwear (the extremely sensible, non-sexy type); a king-sized exceptionally realistic dildo with one of those suction cups at the end so it could be mounted onto a wall; a rosary; a Buddha head; a handheld mirror; some tarot cards; a handkerchief; and most strangely of all, an actual human skull - with a full set of teeth glistening menacingly, which made Ward want to scream out in terror when he realised what it was (the pants were draped over the skulls skeletal features, concealing most of it from view).

Later that night, when Officer's Ward and Nicol had finished their shifts and gone home to their young wives to be comforted and counselled and (most likely) hit the hard liquor, Chief Inspector Pommery sent the human skull, along with the rest of the bizarre artefacts, to the local crime lab for testing. He wasn't certain, but he had the niggling suspicion that the skull, along with everything else, would indeed belong to Alice Doyle. What that would mean exactly, he didn't want to contemplate. Had this sick sonofabitch actually dug up his sister in order to retrieve her emancipated head? If that were true, then that was another charge added to the growing list of felonies this bastard was culpable of. How he had expected to get away with it was beyond him. Or maybe, just maybe, he'd never expected to get away with any of it in the first place... He simply didn't care. If that were the case, then they were dealing with one exceedingly dangerous individual. One not seen in these parts since the days of Bible John and Fred and Rose West - who used to hide the bodies of their victims under their front porch.

Among the madness of macabre collectibles, was the purse Pommery had requested. Inside the purse, exactly as described, was the passport photograph of Alice Doyle's father, staring blankly at the camera with wide blue eyes reminiscent of his daughter's.

Pommery had placed the picture on his desk where he was examining it with a magnifying glass. Earlier that evening, he had placed a call to Prestwick barracks and effectively passed the buck of bad news onto Lieutenant Colonel Clarkson, who had taken the news sombrely but proactively at least.

Pommery stared down at the face of the man he'd never seen before. Was this man now his prime suspect in the murder of Alice Doyle? A case so old that it'd long since been archived and forgotten. Making up his mind, he reached out for his phone again and placed a call to the Barrhead police station. The fellow in charge there was a man by the name of Jagger (like the sticky-fingered rocker from his youth).

Inspector Christopher Jagger was a relatively young man, twenty years Pommery's junior, but still considered relatively experienced in his field.

Pommery had worked closely with him on a number of cases over the years - most notably the case of young Jessica Parish and her sadistic, Satan-worshipping boyfriend, Matthew Knowles, who beat her to death with a bicycle pump at her sixteenth birthday party, then hid her body in the bike shed at the back of his garden.

The reason he was calling him now, however, was to call in a long-overdue favour he'd been saving for a rainy day such as this one.

'Hello. Barrhead Station,' came the pleasant voice from the other end.

'Hello. this is Chief Inspector Pommery, from Neilston. I wish to speak to Inspector Jagger, if he's available?'

'One moment please.' She popped the phone on hold and a low humming noise ensued for several seconds after.

'Inspector Jagger,' came a much firmer voice down the line.

'Chris. Hello, it's Bill Pommery here.'

'Bill, good to hear from you. Still successfully evading retirement, I see.'

'I've got a few years left in me yet. Listen, I wanted to ask you for a favour.'

'Well, as I recall, I do owe you one...'

'You do. It's regarding an old case we've just recently reopened here in Neilston. A young girl by the name of Doyle - she lived over in your neck of the woods. Do you remember?'

'Can't say I do. How long ago was that?'

'It'll be ten years now.'

'Crikey, you expect me to remember that long ago? I can't even remember the names of my wife's brothers half the time or what I had for breakfast yesterday, never mind cases that've been gathering dust for ten years!'

Pommery chuckled appreciatively. 'I guess I'm lucky my wife is an only child.'

'So, what about this case then?'

'I need you to check the current owner of a house over on Gary Crescent - number seventeen - and I need a list of tenants going back the last three decades.'

'Sure thing. Do you have a perp in mind?'

'Potentially. I've got a picture, but no name. Keep an eye out for the name 'Doyle'. The kids took their mother's last name and she's listed as being single and passed away a few years ago, but if I'm right, there was a male cohabitating that property with the mother before the son was born.'

'And you think this guy had something to do with the girl's death?'

'That's what we're thinking. Can you give me a ring if you find something?'

'I'll do you one better; I'll fax you over the complete list of tenants once I have it.'

'Thanks, Chris. I appreciate it.'

'No problem. Consider us even. Take it easy.'

Pommery hung up the phone. Next he placed a call to the Scottish Police Authority Forensic Services over in Gartcosh. A young man by the name of Edward Charpentier had been dealing with the case, and he had the man's desk extension on speed dial. 'Eddie', as he liked to be called, was known as 'The

Carpenter' among police officers. Like Pommery's late grandfather, Eddie Charpentier's mother had emigrated to Scotland from France. The young man could speak fluently in both languages, among his many other talents. Pommery knew that in return Eddie and his team probably referred to him by some champagne related pun, but he didn't mind; he was well used to that by now (his nickname during his time at the police training college in Jackton had been 'Bubbles').

'You've reached Eddie. I'm not at my desk right now, but please leave a message and I'll get back to you when I can,' came the recording from the answering machine. Pommery hung up the phone without leaving a message - he figured the kid would call him when he had something anyway.

Just as he was about to get up and make himself a strong cup of coffee, the phone rang again. He sighed deeply and settled back into his chair.

'Chief Inspector Pommery,' he said wearily.

'Hello there. My name is Pamela Kelso.'

'Good evening, ma'am. How can I help you?'

'I understand two officers dropped by the hotel yesterday to speak to my father? Well, he's been highly agitated since they left - I have no problem telling you - acting quite peculiarly indeed. I haven't seen him like this since Rowland, his horse, died three summers ago this June. Anyway, what I was calling to tell you - he spoke to me about it this morning - he told me to tell you that it might not've been an older man at all that he saw that night... He now thinks it could in fact have been a younger man instead! I'm assuming this means

190

something to you? Because I don't have the faintest idea what he's talking about. His memory's been getting a lot worse lately. I keep telling him it's those pills that the doctor gave to him. They're giving him all sorts of unpleasant side effects, you see. I've caught him walking around the hotel twice now without his trousers on! Mercy! It's a miracle one of the guests didn't catch him! Anyway, I just thought I should call to let you know what he told me,' and without waiting for Pommery to reply, the woman hung up on him.

Bewildered, Pommery stared at the receiver in silence, then slowly placed it on the hook. Then, as if by some form of cosmic duality, the phone rang again not a second after he'd put it down. Without taking his hand off the handset, he lifted the phone to his ear again and answered it.

'Chief Inspector Pommery.'

'Bill, It's Chris again. I'm glad I caught you before you went home! Listen, I've had a look at the list of tenants who've lived at the address you gave me, going all the way back to the fifties.'

'You did? Thank you for doing that, I appreciate the help.'

'Anyway, listen, you were right – there was a woman living at that address by the name of Cynthia Doyle. She was at the property from eighty-one until she died in oh-four. And, like you said, there was a man registered as living at the same address for three of those years until he died in eighty-nine. If what you told me earlier is correct, then this guy, James Talbert, who was living with Cynthia Doyle, can't have been the man that you're after as he died eight years before it happened!'

Pommery drew a deep breath through his nose. 'Thanks Chris. You've been a big help…'

'No problem. Are you sure you're looking at the right leads here? Seems to me like you're barking up the wrong tree with this one.'

'You could be right,' Pommery accepted. 'It seems this case is wide open. It's been a hell of a day. You wouldn't believe what we found at this guy's house earlier… We could be dealing with our very own Norman Bates.'

'You don't say? Well, maybe it's time to dust off the old golf clubs and get the hell out of Dodge while you still can. Retirement must be looking more tempting that ever.'

'It certainly is. Anyway, thanks for the help on this. I'll let you get on - it's getting late.'

'No problem. If there's anything else you need… you know what to do.'

He heard the phone click at the other end, then the long droning hum of the dial tone. That night, when Bill Pommery finally crept into bed beside his sleeping wife, he pictured Alice Doyle's skull and the headless skeleton underground that had parted with it.

Chapter 28
Burnt Eggs and Toast

The next morning, Pommery awoke with a cold layer of sweat gripping his night-shirt. His wife, Mandy, was still snoring softly beside him - a peaceful dreamless sleep that he envied her of madly. He checked his bedside clock and the small digital screen blinked '07:32' at him. Today was the day he'd either have to charge the man or release him. He had full confidence in Eddie, and his young team of specialists, that they would come back to him with some positive matches. But still, something at the back of his mind was troubling him and he couldn't quite put his finger on what it was.

It was Sunday, and on Sunday mornings he didn't work. Mandy would want to spend the morning in the garden with him, tending to their begonias and checking if their vegetables were ripe for picking (it was getting towards that time). He however was eager to get himself back to the station.

As she stirred and rolled toward him, he put his arm around her neck and cradled her snuggly on his chest.

'What time is it?' she murmured, still shrugging off the last vestiges of sleep.

'It's not yet eight,' he replied gently, kissing her warm forehead and breathing in the pleasant fragrance of her hair.

'That's good. I'll put on some breakfast.'

'You just stay where you are. I'll see to it.' Pommery swung a thin leg from under the covers and pulled himself from out beneath her. 'Go back to sleep, love. I'll bring breakfast up for you in a bit.' He looked himself out a simple plaid shirt from his dresser and an old pair of jeans to go with it, then headed down the stairs. His daughter was still asleep (and likely would be until noon, given her track record of Sundays). He hadn't heard her come in last night, but he assumed it'd been late. Despite being in his early sixties now, he tried to remind himself that he was young once, too.

Down in the kitchen, he donned a scabby pair of trainers then got to work on the breakfast. He ran the kettle under the tap and stuck it over the hot stove, then he fired two bits of pumpkin loaf bread into the toaster and started on the eggs. He reached into the fridge and grabbed the carton of OJ from the top shelf, removed three free-range eggs and broke them into the frying pan. Today was going to be a big day for him, and a big day called for a big feed in the morning. While he waited for the eggs to whiten, he poured himself a cold glass of orange juice and sat down at the kitchen table.

He wondered if today would be one of those career-defining days that he would be remembered for. A homicide in Neilston was troubling enough, but now to add grave robbing to the mix as well was something that would keep the papers talking for weeks. Perhaps it would even make the national news and he'd be interviewed for STV Scotland and have a nice little slot on the telly around teatime after Countdown. He'd sit and watch it with his wife and his daughter, and they'd congratulate him on a job well done in catching the sick son-of-a-bitch responsible. Once he got the phone call from Eddie, that would hopefully reach the station that morning, then he'd have the proof he needed to put this case to bed. What troubled him, however, was the as of yet unexplained demise of Alice Doyle, his chief suspect's late older sister.

He had two separate cases connected by one long ago incident that seemed to set everything else into motion. If there was only one killer in each instance, who happened to be the man he had in his custody right now, then that would certainly be a lot easier than looking for some unknown assailant somehow connected to Alice Doyle and, depending on which of the hotel manager's recollections you believed, was either old enough to be her father, or young enough to be her brother. But the prints didn't match... That was the one thing that didn't add up. If it had been Kieran Doyle in the first instance, then his prints would be in the car alongside his sister's.

The toaster popped beside him and he jolted in his chair, forgetting he'd put it on in the first place. He went over to the frying pan and flipped the eggs onto their yokes (Mandy liked them burnt to a cinder on either side). When they were ready, he lay the eggs and the toast on two separate plates and made his wife a pot of tea to go with it. Although he usually got two eggs and she only one, today he suspected he would have to turn the tables in order to soften the blow of his skipping out on their usual Sunday routine.

Mandy wasn't happy, of course. 'You only get one morning off a week!' she'd yelled. 'You need to rest, or you'll give yourself a heart attack!' But this was a day he simply couldn't sit at home and wait for noon to strike before bursting into action. He wanted to be at his desk ready for the call from Eddie's team to come in, so he could be the one to charge Kieran Doyle himself, and see that stupefied look on his miserable face.

He left his wife still in bed eating breakfast with a menacing scowl splaying on her face.

'I'll be back early tonight. I promise!' he said, as he closed the door behind him. He'd removed the plaid shirt and jeans and donned his crispy white uniform, complete with the three diamond brooches on the shoulder, displaying his rank. By the time he made it to the station it was approaching nine o'clock and he smiled, knowing the Forensic Services Lab likely didn't open until at least 10am on a Sunday. He'd have plenty of time to get himself organised and perhaps catch up on some paperwork before the phone calls started coming in.

When the clock on the monitor of his computer showed 10:54, his phone rang for the first time that morning. He answered - it was The Carpenter.

Chapter 29
Burke and Hare

Eddie Charpentier and his team of young whizz kids had confirmed what Pommery had suspected all along: the skull, along with the rest of the artefacts found on the Grey's farm, had belonged to Alice Doyle - meaning that there was likely a headless skeleton buried under the girl's headstone in Neilston cemetery. But most shockingly of all (and the proverbial final nail in the coffin) was the confirmation of DNA belonging to Kieran Doyle found on Mrs Gwendolyn Becker's body, confirming that the sick son-of-a-bitch had murdered the poor woman after all.

Now it was Bill Pommery's time to shine. Once he'd hung up, he turned to Sergeant Tom Winley, who was sat at the desk nearest the door.

'We got him,' he said with a self-assured grin.

Sergeant Winley got up from his desk and followed Pommery through to the holding cells. Kieran Doyle was sat on the bed watching them come in.

'Well, Mr Doyle, it looks like you won't be staying with us much longer after all.'

'You're releasing me?' He perked up at the words.

'Quite the opposite. Kieran Doyle, I hereby charge you with the murder of Gwendolyn Becker. You do not have to say anything. But it may harm your defence if you do not mention when questioned something which you later rely on in court. Anything you do say may be given in evidence used against you.'

Kieran's eyes widened as the older man continued.

'You may contact a lawyer, if you wish. You will be arraigned at Glasgow High Court of Justiciary tomorrow morning, then remanded into custody to await your trial.'

'Where will they take me?' Kieran asked, starting to look highly concerned.

'My best guess would be Deepwood, up near Fort William. But if they don't want you there then it'll be Shotts. But that's for the Crown to decide now. You're out of our hands.'

'I want a phone call.' He was standing up now and glaring at them through the bars - each hand gripped around the rusted metal.

'Sergeant Winley here will arrange that for you, once we've got your charge sheet drawn up.'

They left Kieran Doyle alone in his holding cell and made their way back out into the corridor. *A lot of good lawyers will do him with evidence like that piled up against him*, Pommery thought to himself as they walked. *Maybe with a really good one they could get his sentence shaved by a year or two, but the actuality is, Kieran Doyle is looking at spending the rest of his life behind bars whether he likes it or not. We have his DNA on the body of Mrs Becker, as well as the host of other sick items we've found that incriminate him.*

For now, Pommery's attention was turned to the other grisly task he had lined up for that morning – the matter of Alice Doyle's partially disseminated remains. He'd have to phone the undertaker over at the Neilston Cemetery and get a team out there to assist him. He wavered as to whether Officer's Ward and Nicol would be the best men for the job, then decided that this kind of thing was part and parcel of being a police officer and there was no better time than now to get their dicks wet, so to speak. Lord knew he'd seen some grisly things during his time on the force, and these two young officers would have to take it as it comes, like he did when he was their age.

After he'd phoned Donald Burke, who owned Burke and Sons Funeral Directors, and informed him of the situation at the cemetery, he radioed for Officer Nicol, and instructed him and Officer Ward to get over there immediately. He had another matter to attend to while that was going on.

***

'What did he want?' Ward asked, once Nicol was off his radio.

'I've got good news and bad news,' he replied, taking a drink of his double-shot cappuccino - they'd parked up for coffee outside his wife's delicatessen.

200

Officer Ward had a croissant and cinnamon bun as well, as he'd skipped breakfast that morning.

'Okay, give me the good news first then,' he said, taking a big sugary bite of his cinnamon bun.

'They got news back from The Carpenter at the lab. Said Doyle's DNA was all over that Becker woman, so we've pinned the son-of-a-bitch for the murder.'

'That's great news!' he replied, slurping down some coffee and wiping his mouth on the sleeve of his white shirt. 'It had to be him - the guy's a fucking weirdo!'

'Well, then there's the bad news,' Nicol continued. 'They've matched the skull we found at the house to Alice Doyle, so Chief wants us down at the graveyard to oversee the digging…'

'You're joking?'

'Afraid not.'

'What kind of shit detail is that?' He slammed the takeaway coffee cup on his leg and the drink splashed out and burned his hand. 'Shit! Look what you made me do now!'

'Come on let's get this over with,' Nicol said, placing his own drink in the round holder between them.

Officer Nicol started the engine of the old BMW squad car and they pulled out into the quiet Sunday traffic of Neilston town centre. It was approaching 11am and most folks would be piling into church right about now, meaning their visit wouldn't remain a secret for long. *'With any luck'*, Officer Ward thought, *'we can park down the street and wait until the church doors*

*had closed and Sunday mass had started, minimising the
likelihood of being detected'.* As it turned out, that'd been
wishful thinking.

The first person to spot their car arriving at the
cemetery was a boy around the age of five. He pointed
over at them as Nicol pulled the car into the curb and
his parents looked up and got a good eyeful of them
arriving. The couple then preceded to nudge the
couple next to them, who looked up and spotted them
next.

'Well, so much for staying incognito,' Ward
sighed, as he stepped out of the squad car.

Thankfully, by the time they'd done the two-
minute walk up to the churchyard, most of the
congregation had disappeared into the building. The
few stragglers that were left were finishing off their
cigarettes and stubbing them out beneath their feet.
The Chief had told Nicol over the radio that he'd
arranged for Mr Burke the undertaker to meet them at
the steps at the far side of the church – below which,
the graveyard stretched out in all directions. A gothic,
macabre, creepy sort of place, that Officer Ward had no
desire to enter alone.

The large archway at the bottom of the stairs
served as the entrance to the necropolis. The
inscription along the stone read, 'Spes Illorum
Immortalitate Plena Est', which Ward had once been
told meant something like *'their hope is full of
immortality'.* They spotted the old man waiting for
them as they rounded the first corner of the large
church. He was stood at the bottom of the steps,
wearing a dark grey jacket and cap to keep out the

rain. He looked to Ward to be pushing into his seventies – pretty soon he would be handing over the reins of the business to his sons and getting on with whatever it was funeral directors did in their retirement. The elder son had come along with him and was stood by his side. He was tall and thin and still in his twenties, or possibly early thirties, not too far off the age of the two police offers now approaching him. In his hands, he appeared to be holding some form of large hammer.

'Good morning,' croaked the old man as they arrived by his side.

Ward nodded at them in turn.

'Dark business you've got me on today. Dark business indeed. Digging up the dead is not something I take lightly. I put them in the ground, that's all, not the other way around.'

'I apologise,' Ward replied. 'Unfortunately, in this case, it's necessary, or we wouldn't be troubling you.'

'Last time I was asked to do something like this was in nineteen-seventy-nine. A boy by the name of Gibson. Wanted for murder he was. They had to use bite marks from his teeth to string him to the murder of his sister. Poor woman was near bit through to the bone. Turns out, he never done it in the end. Was some drifter fella from Wales who'd met her down the Traveller's Rest. Killed her in the back of his car - after they'd gotten down to it in the backseat that was. Since then, I'm wary of digging up folks who've no need of being disturbed. It's no good disturbin' the dead.'

'Do you know where we're going?' Nicol asked, once the old man stopped talking.

'Well I should do, shouldn't I? I was the one who put her in the ground in the first place. Follow me, it's not too far from here. Her mother is plotted next to her - did that one more recently. Gavin here will do the digging.'

Mr Burke and his son Gavin led them through the large gothic archway and then headed east, into the deeper recesses of the cemetery. Neither of the officers felt comfortable with what they were about to do. Ward distracted himself by thinking that soon he would be rolling croissant dough and feeding the sourdough starters in his wife's delicatessen, and all of this would be behind him. It was nasty business this and one that he wanted to be done with as soon as humanly possible.

Just as they were approaching the headstone that Mr Burke had pointed out to them, the rain started falling again and heavier this time too. Ward popped the collar on his luminescent jacket and shivered – he wasn't sure whether it was the cold or what they were about to do that had caused it.

'There she is,' Burke said, walking towards a small headstone that was centred amongst a collection of large tombs. As he got closer, he bent lower, as if scrutinizing the ground beneath his feet.

'That's been shifted, that has!' he barked, leaning over the soil in front of the headstone. 'Not recently mind you, but someone, other than myself, has been at this. Just look at the grass there – its uneven.'

Ward and Nicol arrived at his side. 'Yes, well… that's what we'd expected.'

'Graverobbers in these parts? I'd never... Who'd do such a thing?'

'We believe it's the brother,' Nicol offered. 'We have him in custody at the station.'

'You're telling me this boy dug up his own sister?'

'He's highly unstable. But don't worry, we've just been told this morning that he'll likely be behind bars for a very long time, so he won't be disturbing anymore graves anytime soon.'

'Well, let's get this business over with,' Burke muttered, nodding at his son to start the digging.

Fifteen minutes later, the young Mr Burke struck wood beneath the dirt. He'd heaped the soil behind them, and the large pile was approaching waist height. The young man poked his head out of the hole and called out to his father.

'Someone's been at this all right. The grave liner's been smashed!'

Ward peered into the hole and saw large concrete shards protruding from the dirt. 'What the hell is it?' he asked, confused by what he was seeing.

'That there was the grave liner,' replied old man Burke. They stop the coffins from collapsing under the weight of the earth and keep the interior's nice and dry - but looks like someone's been at this one with a sledgehammer. In the old days they were made of wood, but now we use concrete – it lasts longer, you see.'

'What do we do now?' asked Nicol.

'Well, I guess it's made our job a bit easier,' he motioned to the large hammer that was strewn on the grass beside the large pile of dirt.

'I'll need a hand with these slabs,' said the young man from the hole. Ward looked over at Officer Nicol then lowered himself into the grave alongside Gavin.

After ten gruelling minutes of prying the large slabs from the mud, then heaving them over the side, they had removed the last shard of shattered concrete from above the coffin. Gavin jabbed the spade into the earth and the sound of wood beneath could be heard. Ward collapsed against the side of the grave and wiped the cold beads of sweat mixed with rain from his brow.

'Still intact,' Gavin observed, prodding through the earth with his spade.

'How long do they last?' Ward asked, still catching his breath.

'A solid pine coffin will last ten to fifteen years, before it starts to rot away. Looks like this one has started to fall away a bit, but the main structure's still there.'

'What about the body?' asked Nicol, looking cagey. This was a question he didn't like asking but felt it pertinent at a time like this.

'Nothing but bones...' It was the crooked old crypt keeper who replied. He had walked around the hole and was now leaning awkwardly against the headstone. Ward pictured the skull from the bedroom with the underwear draped over it and he shivered (this time it definitely wasn't the cold that had caused it).

Gavin used the edge of his shovel to scrape the remaining dirt away from the coffin. Once he was done, he hoisted himself from the hole and stood beside it, assessing the work he'd done. 'Want me to do the honours, pops?'

'I'll do it,' replied the old man, gravely. 'Here, hand me that shovel, will you?' He used the arm of his son to lower himself into the hole. Once inside, he got down on his knees and wiped away a smattering of dirt from the lid with his sleeve. He began scanning the edges of the coffin gently with his fingers, then hoisted it open with one giant heave. The rain had just about stopped now - only a few straggling drops were still falling from the sky. Mr Burke wiped his brow with his sleeve and let out a painful sigh at what was inside the coffin.

Ward approached the edge hesitantly, not wanting to look, but at the same time finding himself unable to look away. Nicol too, was clambering for a better look by his side. 'What is it?' Ward asked, unwillingly.

Mr Burke got slowly to his knees and stood aside, allowing a full view of the coffin behind him. All four men realised the problem immediately – a problem that added yet another sinister twist to this troubling tale. The coffin, still relatively intact despite ten years beneath the soil, was empty…

Chapter 30
Looking Back

Kieran sat staring through the rusted bars of his cell and thought about what was coming to him. He had hoped that his look of incredulity when the Chief Inspector had charged him with the murder had seemed genuine. He had of course expected this all along. No matter how careful you were in matters such as these, you always leave something - some trace, some fragment, some fibre of your being that is imprinted on the scene and impossible to recover no matter how hard you try. Modern forensics had reached the point where even the most careful of killers were starting from a disadvantage.

He wondered what piece of him had been found. What fragment they'd uncovered. He'd worn gloves of course, so fingerprints were out of the question. He'd covered as much of his skin as he could and donned a ski mask to prevent discarded hairs falling from his head. He'd returned to the scene of the crime with the daughter, Claire, and left as much bodily evidence as he could to muddy the waters. But still they'd found him there, between the lines; on her body, where he'd slipped the knife from the Grey's kitchen into that gullet while she'd slept. He'd covered her mouth with his gloved hand, suppressing the scream, and she'd bitten down into his forefinger. Perhaps it was her teeth that had given away his secret - one of many.

Mrs Becker got what she had coming to her in the end. If it weren't for her and her dumb fuck of a husband, his darling sister would never have fled from the car that night. Never have ran away from him as he tried to comfort her the way he had done. In truth, Alice was the only person Kieran had ever loved. He'd loved every inch of her. Every beautiful hair on her immaculate head. He'd loved the way she'd smile at him while she was reading his favourite stories to him at night. He'd loved the way she smelled when he'd sunk his head into her ample bosom and slept as peacefully as a baby deep in its cot. He'd loved to hear the sound of her singing in the bathroom as she showered, and he'd to spend the rest of his day whistling the very same tune.

When he'd gotten a little older and the adoration had grown into strong sexual attraction, he'd use anything he could find of hers to satisfy himself while she was away. He had a collection of discarded underwear that he'd removed from her dirty clothes hamper. He'd stolen illicit sex toys he'd found in her room, before returning them to her drawer before she could notice their absence. He'd loved her more than he loved anything else in the world, and his one wish had been to consummate that love so she could love him in return. But before he'd had the chance to show her how he felt, her life had ended.

He'd been distraught (stunned might have been a better word). So stunned in fact, that he'd lost all sense of meaning to his life. Taking care of their mother was the last thing on his mind. He didn't change her, rarely fed her, became all but oblivious to her incessant whining. Eventually it got to the stage where he could no longer even look at her. She wasn't a person to him anymore. Not even the slightest semblance of a person (if she ever had been). She was simply an extension of that damned electric chair she wheeled around the house in day and night. Always whining, always wanting, always something wrong.

He killed her on a Tuesday with a pillow from her own bedroom. He wouldn't dare use one of the precious pillows belonging to his dear sister that still lay on the bed where she'd slept, and still emitted the last vestiges of her scent (though it was fading). With every passing day, it was fading. With every climax, every breath of her soiled cotton knickers, her presence got smaller. She was disappearing from that place. Disappearing with the wind and leaving him alone again.

It had been an accident, the night that she died. A misunderstanding. A simple mistake on her part that had cost her, her life. It was he who was with her of course, near the end. He who'd been sat in the car with her as those bastards chased them through the snow and then left them in a ditch to die.

He'd planned to surprise her. He spent that afternoon walking from their small home in Barrhead

to where Alice worked, on the Montgreenan Estate.
The walk had taken him until dark, and then when
he'd arrived, he'd waited patiently in the hotel lobby
for her to finish.

Upon finishing, she had of course been delighted
to see him - at least that was how he had perceived her
reaction (although, she did seem slightly mad that he'd
walked so far in the dark as it was approaching
midnight by the time he'd got there). They'd gotten
into her car after scraping the excess snow off the
windows, turned on the engine and the heating,
waited for the windscreen to defrost for five minutes,
then set off for home with their teeth chattering in their
skulls.

They hadn't even left the Montgreenan Estate
when they'd seen the car careen around the corner,
headlights blinding them in the distance. At first, they
were confused as to what exactly was happening.
Alice assumed the car had been full of hotel guests
making their way back, most likely intoxicated, after a
night out in Irvine or Glasgow. When they'd skidded
their car in the middle of the road, turned and made to
follow them with their horn blaring and lights
flashing, Alice had panicked.

She should have stopped the car, pulled over to
the side, let them pass and get on with harassing
someone else. Instead, Alice slammed on the
accelerator, wheels skidding in the snow. When she
lost control, they veered off the road and into a tree, by
a small milestone that was jutting out the earth like a
gravestone nearby.

After the car stopped, they'd looked around just in time to see the other car smash into the back of them, with a deafening crunch that threw them into the dashboard. Alice was hurt (it was her neck). She'd been thrown forward so violently in the crash that she'd sustained some sort of injury to her spine.

As the car behind them began to reverse away, Kieran made to get out and go after them, but Alice protested. She was holding her neck with both hands and was bent awkwardly over the steering wheel. He'd shifted over in his seat and was trying to comfort her, but it wasn't helping. She was crying and in pain. The girl he loved so dearly had been hurt and it was killing him to watch her suffer like this. He tried kissing her on the arms and on her shoulders, all in an effort to comfort her. He moved up to her cheek and the side of her mouth and she must have gotten a fright.

He hadn't meant to scare her. He simply wanted to show her how much she meant to him. She recoiled, still holding her neck and screamed at him to get off her. She'd misunderstood his intentions. He wasn't trying to hurt her. He wanted to comfort her and shower her with his love. He'd tried again and she'd balked at him. She pushed the car door open with her shoulder and ran from him. *What was she doing?* He didn't understand. She needed to come back so he could explain what he was doing and that he loved her. He loved her more than anyone or anything and she needed to know that.

He chased her through the snow, along the winding roads of the estate; all the time calling her name, but she wouldn't stop and listen. She threw herself over the wooden fence and fled into the forest that bordered the hotel grounds - reluctantly he followed her. He didn't want to make it seem like he was chasing her - he just wanted to catch up so he could explain what he was doing. *Why wasn't she listening?* She needed to slow down, she could get herself hurt or lost or abducted by some stranger and then she would be taken from him forever - he couldn't let that happen.

He was at last managing to gain on her when it happened; so suddenly; so abrupt; a cry and she was gone. There was no way for either of them to have foreseen it. At first, he couldn't understand what had happened. *Where had she gone?* She was there one moment, not twenty yards in front of him, then gone the next, as if she'd vanished into thin air.

When he arrived at the exact place where she'd disappeared, he almost toppled over himself. He grabbed a branch and somehow managed to stop himself from falling. It was a ravine. An extremely dark, extremely steep and extremely dangerous ravine. She must have fallen over the side. He called her name; yelled out for her, cried for her, told her he loved her, told her he couldn't live without her, but it was no good. Alice was gone.

***

With his mind reeling in mangled shock and disbelief, Kieran had staggered backwards and fallen on the snow-covered ground. He'd sat there, staring at the place where his sister had just been standing, for an immeasurable amount of time. Eventually, as daylight started to gradually break above him, he started to move again. He was frozen to the bone and time had seemed to slow to a standstill. His thoughts moved in heady circles, never becoming clear or apparent. A car had crashed into the back of them. Alice was hurt. He'd tried to comfort her, and she'd ran. Now Alice was gone. Fallen over the edge. Never to return. He spoke the words, but they didn't make sense to him. *Alice is gone? Alice can't be gone... it's not possible.* She'd always been there for him. She was the only person he knew in this cold lonely world that they lived in. What would he do now without Alice? Where did this leave him?

He'd seriously considered throwing himself into the ravine before finally turning away and walking back slowly towards the road; still fixed in an almost trance like state of fading disbelief and burgeoning despair. He'd walked without knowing where his legs were taking him. Through the snow, which was piled up to his knees, towards home, if there still was still a home to go back to; would there ever be a home again? Who would read his stories to him now? Cook for him? Take care of their mother? Who would he yearn for in the middle of the night when it was all he could do not to slip into her room and get into bed beside her?

***

The next few years had been a very lonely time for him. After the police officer had come and confirmed they'd found his sister's body, all hope that she'd gotten away had faded and he'd slipped into a deep and very dark depression. He'd killed their mother, almost without feeling. What feelings did he have left? None that he could attest to, other than longing and despair.

After the funeral (which had been small and arranged by his great aunt Sarah, who he'd never met before), Kieran collected what savings his mother had amassed (a surprising amount, considering the apparent poverty they lived in - a man named James Talbert had left her a considerable amount of money when he'd died - money that now transferred to Kieran). There were never any questions about how she had died. Her breathing had simply given up on her, which he'd heard was a common occurrence for those with afflictions such as these.

A few weeks later, he took what he needed and left his life in Barrhead behind him. After a month on the road, walking during the day and sleeping in bus shelters and countryside bothys during the night, he'd found himself in Aberdeen, at a small pub named Ma Cameron's, that had a plaque declaring it the oldest pub in town, dating all the way back to 1746.

He'd ordered himself a nip from the oldest bottle of whiskey they had (a Bruichladdich '64, which set him back £30 per measure). After he sank his first, he ordered himself another one. After ten minutes, a man pulled up a barstool and sat down next to him. He was old - perhaps in his sixties. He said his name was

Ramon and upon recognising that Kieran's accent wasn't Aberdonian, he asked what he was doing in these parts. He told him he was just passing through.

'We could use a sturdy man like you on the rigs,' the old man had told him. 'Good money too - if you don't mind a little seasickness.'

Kieran told him that he was interested and a week later he found himself on a helicopter flying out to the Forties oil field, approximately 110 miles north east of Aberdeen, where he'd managed to land himself a three-month contract as a roughneck (or floorhand) on a rig, thanks to Ramon's recommendation.

Despite having to sleep in a room that measured barely six feet across, with three other men who routinely snored themselves to sleep, he found his time on the rig to be congenial. He stayed there for two years in all, frequently requesting that his time back on the mainland be cut short. His superiors seemed to like this and swiftly extended his working contract by a further eighteen months. What little money he made he spent on whiskey and prostitutes; sometimes women, sometimes men, he didn't have a preference. None of them were Alice, and that's all he really wanted.

One night, while visiting a local brothel, known as Hannigan's, he'd found the man beneath him unresponsive, after an intense but satisfying session. He just lay there on the rickety metal bed, not moving. At first, he'd been confused by the man's inactivity - he tried to shake him, but when he wouldn't wake, he panicked and ran. A week later, he would read in a national newspaper that a known prostitute was asphyxiated in one of Aberdeen's most notorious brothels.

He fled Aberdeen that night and made his way south again - once more relying on bus shelters and bothys for shelter during the nights. After several weeks, roaming town to town, he found himself in Glasgow. The big city was brimming with young hungry debutantes, just like him, looking for cheap fucks and cheaper alcohol to sprawl in. He found himself a couch to spend his nights, after meeting a girl at a nightclub, called The Shed, in the southside. She wasn't what he would deem as attractive, being somewhat overweight and a fair few years older, but she was happy enough to let him stay in her flat, as long as he helped her out with the occasional fuck when she was shit-faced and feeling nasty.

Within a month, he felt the need to be on the road again, this time making his way west, closer and closer to the small town in which he'd been raised (and in which his sister Alice rested peacefully beneath the dirt).

On the morning he arrived back in Barrhead, he visited his old home, which had remained unoccupied and abandoned in his absence. His newspapers were still there, and so were his clothes and the rest of his belongings. And so, he was pleased to discover, were all of Alice's possessions as well. He basked in them, rolling himself in her old t-shirts and underwear and smelling her pillow - which still contained the faintest fragrance that had refused to part with the cotton. Rather than comforting him, he found the scent made him angry; outraged in fact. Outraged at the fact that

Alice had been taken from him; outraged at the fact that she had been so young with so much left to live for; outraged at himself for not catching up to her that night; but most of all, he was outraged at whoever had been in the car behind them. Whoever it was that thought it would be fun to play at little game of cat and mouse on the roads covered in snow. Whoever those people were, they would not be alive for much longer. He swore it to himself.

Chapter 31
Red Rabbit and the White Album

The cabin shook as the C-17 transport aircraft touched down hard on the tarmac at RAF Prestwick. The men of Charlie Company, who Noah had hitched a ride with, were removing their neck pillows and taking out earphones, ready for disembarking. The mood on the flight was jovial, with most of those onboard looking forward to spending a whole month back at home with their families. Noah, on the other hand, felt just about the opposite. He'd received the call from his commanding officer not long before he'd boarded the nine-hour flight back to Scotland. His sister, Claire, only twenty-seven years old, had been killed in a car crash near Pitlochry. He'd been granted compassionate leave while he dealt with the proprieties. He had two funerals ahead of him, and neither of the deceased had been enlisted or deployed with him at the time of their deaths.

He'd long suspected his mother had been in the culminating years of a downward spiral that only had one end in sight: something not too dissimilar to the way his father had met *his* bitter end - that is what he'd suspected, anyway. But Claire, she was the most vibrant and colourful person he knew. Granted, they weren't particularly close - well not since everything had changed for them one Christmas a very long time ago - but they certainly weren't strangers. He loved her in a way he'd never showed - or couldn't show. Being affectionate wasn't in his repertoire of emotional responses. Now he would be faced with grief and condolences from the little family he had left - perhaps a few uncles and cousins gathered around boxes as they lowered them into the ground.

While he'd been a little boy growing up in Neilston, he'd never imaged he would be the last Becker to remain standing. The last remaining face without an 'X' marked across it on the family portrait above the fireplace. *What a cruel world we live in.*

He'd seen his fair share of death during his time in the desert - first in Kabul then on to Kandahar; every town looking no different from the last. They'd lost fourteen men in total from his company in his first year in Afghanistan. One of them, Joseph Lipky, he'd just started to get friendly with (they'd swap the CDs and books that they'd brought when they were done with them). Two days after lending him Red Rabbit by Tom Clancy and the White Album by the Beatles, he was dead - ambush attack on an armed convoy that was on its way back from Camp Bastion in the Helmand Province. He was only 21.

As the doors opened and the men began alighting in single file, he imagined the final moments of his mother. When he'd been told that the police suspected murder, at first, he thought he hadn't heard the man correctly.

'Murdered...? But who...?' he'd replied in disbelief. His first point of call would be the police station in Neilston to have a lengthy discussion with whoever was in charge. His mother hadn't been the most likeable woman, a lot of people would agree, but to think that someone would use that as a reason to murder her was unimaginable. Unless it was random - a robbery perhaps? Whatever the circumstances, he needed to know, and he needed to know now. He hadn't realised, but his hand that had been trembling was now gripped so tightly around his MP3 player that it had smashed into pieces in his hands. The plastic screen, now cracked in two, fell to the floor when his grip finally loosened. Somebody needed to pay for what had happened to his family. Someone had killed his mother, which in all likelihood, had led to the death of his sister due to the stress of it or whatever, and that person was going to pay for what they'd done. He swore it to himself.

Chapter 32
Red-Backed Shrike

With Officers Nicol and Ward at the cemetery, dealing with that part of the case, Pommery could now focus his efforts elsewhere - namely, on the thing that'd been bothering him since yesterday. The prints.

Something just didn't add up about the whole 'fingerprints in the car' business. He needed a second opinion, and there was someone he could trust with matters such as these. A man by the name of Irmak. Former detective Mert Irmak was a specialist of sorts in the field of dermatoglyphics. Having long since retired from the police force, the man was now in his seventies and enjoying the peaceful life of a twitcher (or birdwatcher, for those not in the know). It seemed to everyone that he had taken his penchant for looking at magnified images into his retirement; rarely seen without his binoculars and notebook, he spent his days camped out in little shanti huts in the woods, waiting for a peek at his elusive white whale – the Red-Backed Shrike.

Pommery hadn't spoken to him in person in years, but they still exchanged Christmas cards every December, and would continue to do so until one or both of them became too senile to remember.

Mert Irmak was Turkish by birth, though his family had emigrated to the Fair Isle before he'd hit puberty. Regardless of this fact, he still harboured the mistaken belief that Galatasaray football club were *'the best darn football club in Europe'*. Many years ago, when Pommery's own team, St Mirren, had been competing in European football, the two men attended the Galatasaray vs St Mirren match at Love Street ground in Paisley. His team had received an almighty thumping from the Turks - something that Mert never let him forget.

Over the years, there had been the odd occasion when Pommery would consult with Irmak on cases in which we felt his expertise could be of value. Most of the time, Mert was happy to help free of charge, giving the binoculars a rest for an afternoon of police work. Perhaps still being called upon occasionally made him feel needed and that made him feel special, Pommery was grateful either way. He'd placed a phone call to the man as soon as he'd arrived at the police station. Mert, who lived in Comrie, near Crieff, agreed to help if Bill could send him scanned copies of the print sheets via email, which he told him he would do immediately.

'You'd don't sound like yourself, Bill.' Mert observed. 'Sounds like this case has gotten you all riled up...'

'It's a bad one,' Bill agreed. 'A lot for such a small station to deal with, if you know what I mean?'

'Still just the seven of you?' Mert asked.

'Yup. Although it's likely to be eight soon. We've got a young girl transferring from Holland Street. She's just turned nineteen. I had liked to think Neilston would be a nice little starter town for her – somewhere to learn the ropes away from all the madness. Now I'm not so sure…'

'That bad, is it? Well, if nothing else, at least there might be a little eye candy around the office.'

'I'm a happily married man, and you know it.' The two men laughed and ended the call with hearty goodbyes. Pommery got to work scanning the print sheets immediately. He wanted this wrapped up as soon as humanly possible.

Chapter 33
The Cat and the Mouse

It took Kieran the best part of two years to unravel the mystery of who'd been in the car behind them. He had the newspaper clippings from the day they'd found the car and the day they'd found her body. He had another clipping (that he hadn't shown Claire) from the day the police had linked the abandoned car to the body found in the ravine. In the end it had been the red paint left on the rear bumper of his sister's Citroen Debut that had given the game away.

He had visited every garage in the East Renfrewshire area, asking the owners about any red cars that had been brought in over the last couple of years that showed signs of damage to the front bumper, possibly from a collision. This of course had been fruitless. There had been hundreds of cars in the area with damage matching that description. The time frame was too big. Too much time had passed since he'd started his search.

Then he'd received a glimmer of hope in the most improbable of places: Neilston - the very next town over - from the owner of a local car garage on Kingston Road called Brittle and Sons. When Kieran had arrived, and asked what he came to ask, the man had given him the same spiel about how he'd seen lots of cars fitting that description. But when Kieran turned to leave, the man held out his hand and stopped him. He fixed him with a grave and uncertain look and said, 'This wouldn't happen to be about that Doyle girl now would it?'

The owner, Mike Brittle, then went on to describe, in vivid detail, the time Frank Becker had visited his garage with a dent in the front of his red Ford Mondeo, roughly the size of a football.

'Hit a stag, did you?' Mike had asked him at the time.

'Yeah, something like that,' Frank Becker had replied.

Mike had fixed the car up for him, no more questions asked, but he'd seen the blue paint etched into the dents in the fender and he'd seen the article in the newspaper about the abandoned car. He wasn't an overtly clever man by any means, but he was perceptive, and he'd perceived in Mr Becker's eyes a look of fear that had no right to be there when he'd talked to him. It occurred to Mike later, that the fear he'd seen in the man's eyes, perhaps, was the fear of getting caught.

Once Kieran knew who he was dealing with, it didn't take him long to find an address. One of the best things about small towns and local people, was their willingness to give up private information about their fellow residents, all in the name of being neighbourly.

Once he knew where they lived, that's when things started to get interesting.

Initially, he'd had no intention of being rash. He sat back and observed the house for a good long while. Learning who they were and how they went about their lives. It didn't take long for him to realise, that the man and wife that lived there on a permanent basis had both adopted somewhat destructive routines. They lived a dark and miserable existence. Their days, almost with exception, were clouded by an alcohol imbued haze and punctuated by heated arguments that could be heard from the windows and the front door, which was left permanently ajar.

They had no children that he could attest to seeing - although there was the possibility that they were grown and had fled their mother's nest, leaving mum and dad to kill each other in private. Before long, he grew curious about the house that lay adjacent to the Becker's. It sat silent, unperturbed, most likely abandoned. It was much bigger than what he'd be needing but the temptation to investigate the property further overcame him.

Around the far side of the house, he found a bathroom window left ajar. The space was small, but he managed to wiggle his way through it after removing most of his clothes. After spending his first night on the property, he decided to stay. He would need to make some adjustments of course, if he were to be moving temporarily closer to the Becker's. Small towns like Neilston were about keeping up appearances, and he would need to go into the town frequently to get food and supplies. He went to an

outwear store and bought himself a selection of
country attire - no one asked questions when they
assumed you were a man of the land. Next, he used a
large chunk of his inheritance to purchase the second-
hand Land Rover from a dealership in Irvine. The
appearance of money would go some way to insuring
his anonymity - especially from the law.

In the end, he'd been surprised how easy it had
been to hijack another's house. The Grey farm
provided him with ample opportunity to lie in wait,
stalking the Becker's like a lioness stalking two
unknowing gazelles.

***

On the night Frank Becker had died it had been
snowing. He sat in the upper bedroom of the old
house and watched the man drunkenly stumble into
the driver's seat of his red car, then drive zigzaggedly
down the drive and off along the dirt road.

This was his chance. He hurried down the stairs of
the old house, threw on a jacket and jumped into the
Land Rover - which he'd parked out of sight, behind
the crumbling old barn, away from prying eyes.

It didn't take long for him to catch up to Frank
Becker's vehicle, once he'd made it into town. He
didn't know where the man was headed, but he knew
where he was going. This time, he would be the cat
playing with the little mouse.

As the snow grew heavier, Frank maintained a
speed that would likely have caused a crash without
any help from Kieran. He took the slip-road onto the

M77 towards Glasgow. The roads were quiet. The hour was growing late, although it was not yet fully dark. Or perhaps it was the snow-covered hillsides that provided an artificial brightness, tricking the mind into believing it was still day.

When they approached the large roundabout at Stepps, Kieran saw his chance. He manoeuvred to take over, but instead slammed the side of the Land Rover hard against the red Mondeo. Both cars skidded on impact, but Kieran remained in control. The red Mondeo driven by Frank Becker, on the other hand, careened dangerously towards the side, then in a blip in which the car momentarily disappeared, it toppled over the boundary and into the snowy field in a cloud of white. In his rear-view mirror, he watched the car flip and roll like a dead leaf in the wind. Satisfied his work was done, he adjusted the mirror back towards himself and drove off into the night.

Chapter 34
Wood for the Trees

It was early afternoon by the time Mert Irmak got back to Chief Inspector Pommery. Earlier that day, he'd received a troubling update from Officer Ward. The coffin that should've contained the headless remains of Alice Doyle, was now apparently empty. Not a single bone recovered. Someone had stripped the gravesite completely.

Kieran Doyle still sat waiting in his holding cell, where he would sit until tomorrow, the day of his indictment, then Neilston station would be rid of him for good. Pommery was waiting for Officers Nicol and Ward to return so he could begin a new line of questioning when his telephone rang again. It was Mert Irmak – the Red-Backed Shrike.

'Well, you were right,' Mert said, sounding weary. 'The prints are too similar to eliminate the suspect entirely.'

'I know,' Pommery sighed. 'But where does that leave us?'

The line went silent.

'Mert? Are you there?'

'Yes, I'm still here. I've been thinking... I might have seen something like this before.'

'Really? When?'

'A long time ago. It was a young man, similar to the one you have in custody. We had his prints, but we couldn't get an exact match on the ones we'd taken from the scene. It turned out, this young lad, suffered from psoriasis...'

'You mean eczema?'

'Precisely. When it was inflamed, He got rashes on his arms and on his hands and even on his fingers and their tips. These rashes got so bad that they ever so slightly altered the man's fingerprints, leaving us with a false print. We had a doctor, a skin expert - a derma-thingy, what-do-you-call-them - testify in court that it was possible for this condition to temporarily change a person's fingerprints, meaning that the prints we had that weren't an exact match, could be used in evidence to convict, if we could provide a positive diagnosis.'

'And what happened?'

'Well, it turned out that the lad had indeed suffered from the condition the doc had described. In the end, the doc's testimony helped get the guilty verdict, and the young lad was put away for the murder.'

The line went silent as Pommery processed the story.

'Bill? You still there?'

'Yes, I'm here alright, Mert. Y'know, this could be what we've been missing... The reason why none of it

seemed to fit! Mert my friend, I think you might've just
solved a ten-year-old murder case!'

Chapter 35
Blown Rose

Once Frank Becker was dead, Kieran decided it prudent he lay low for a while. He didn't leave the farmhouse for over a month; living off old food tins the Greys had left behind them. There was no electricity or hot water, but he ate everything cold. Cold beans, cold sweetcorn, cold soup, he didn't mind. He was grateful for the sustenance they provided him.

When he finally deemed it safe for himself to re-emerge, he set his sights on another task that needed taking care of. His sister didn't belong by herself in a cold cemetery, rotting beneath the earth. She belonged with him, and he would see to it that she was by his side.

He used the cover of night to aid his bidding. Parking the Land Rover on a small street behind the church and making sure absolutely no one was around before creeping through the archway into the cemetery.

He'd been only sixteen years old when they'd held a small ceremony for Alice in this very location, nearly nine months after she had in fact died. The funeral had been arranged by a lady named Sarah - his mother's aunt - who he'd never met and would not meet again until she'd arranged a similar ceremony for his mother.

He knew the location of the grave by the simple fact that one of the only streetlamps in the cemetery, shone directly over where his sister rested - like a protective shield, simultaneously guiding him towards her and guarding her from harm.

He'd brought a shovel, a sledgehammer, a rope, and a large bin liner - he'd found all four in the battered old shed which sat in the Grey's backyard.

'Don't worry, my love. I'm taking you home,' he whispered, as he approached the familiar headstone protruding silently from the earth. The digging had hardly taken him anytime at all. When he hit the solid lid of the concrete liner, they'd entrapped her in, he reached for the hammer and with three almighty swings, broke the slab in two.

Now he reached for the rope. He tied a firm knot around the smaller part of the lid, then hoisted himself from the hole. Once out, he threw the rope over the thick branch of a nearby tree. He grabbed the rope between his fists, twisted it a few times around his knuckles, then began to heave down, using the branch as a rudimentary pulley.

By the time he'd moved the slab far enough to see the coffin underneath, he was buckled over, gasping for his breath. Once his lungs began to catch up with him, he grabbed the spade and jumped back in the hole. It wasn't long before he'd cleared most of the earth around the top section of the coffin. Thankfully, when his aunt had been selecting his sister's coffin, she had opted for one which allowed the top portion to open separately from the rest of it. This mechanism of course was usually reserved for open casket services, where the family could view their beloved deceased prior to the burial. In Alice's case, of course, this hadn't been an option. Having been left for nine months at the bottom of a ravine - weather, scavengers and natural decomposition all taking their toll - she was in no fit state for public display. (*You look beautiful, my love, beautiful*)

Once the dirt was clear, Kieran stared down at the top of his sister's coffin and smiled. 'Hello, my love,' he sighed, loud enough for a bird to take flight from the nearby tree where it'd been soundly asleep. 'There's no need to worry. I'm going to get you out of there...'

***

Kieran awoke the next morning with a warm feeling of genuine happiness. His sister was safe in the backyard-home at last, after all those years away- and he was now free to return his focus to the matter at hand. The matter of Gwendolyn Becker.

Chapter 36
Small Mercies

He lay in wait. Days passed, weeks went by, months
fell away like autumn leaves from the trees, and before
he knew it, a few years had passed - each day
watching her from afar. She rarely left the house, much
like him, and when she did it was only for the briefest
moment. She'd given up going into town on her own
and had all of her food delivered - every Sunday at
6pm, without fail, the food truck would arrive to
deliver her weakly prescription with a jangling of
liquor bottles and the shuffling of wine.

After a while, he started to think that maybe she
would put an end to it long before he'd get the chance
to. Or perhaps, she'd choke on her own vomit or
topple down the stairs and break her neck and he'd
never know until the ambulance arrived several days
later. She had precious little contact with the outside
world. Nobody knew how she was keeping or how
she spent the long hours of each day (with the
exception of him, who watched her from afar).

So, he waited. Waited for what, he didn't know. But in wait he remained. Then one day it occurred to him: maybe *she* was waiting for *him* to end it for her... Maybe she'd seen him at the window and knew why he was there. Maybe she sat in her living room waiting for footsteps in the kitchen, a shadow in the hallway, and then the cool steel of his blade at her neck to take all her pain away. That's when he decided that it was time to end this for the both of them. He would bring her miserable existence to an end, and if it turned out he would be doing her a favour in the process then so be it. Small mercies, after all, were real and did not occur randomly or merely by coincidence. Now she would be thankful for the small mercy he would grant her.

Chapter 37
Crystals on the Water

When Monday morning came, Bill Pommery could finally drive to work with something to smile about. Today was the day he would drive Kieran Doyle to Glasgow High Court of Justiciary for his arraignment then be rid of him once and for all. Neilston was a small town, a quiet town, a peaceful town, and not somewhere that took kindly to young maniacs interrupting their long-established peace. He'd decided to bring Officer Ward along with him. The young arresting officer would benefit from the experience - not to mention he was strong and fit and a good man to have around if things went haywire.

They loaded Mr Doyle into the van and took their seats in the front - which had a metal partition with a little window in it separating it from the hold. Strangely, Pommery noticed, their prisoner appeared to be in high spirits. For what reason he couldn't fathom. Perhaps he was just happy to be getting out of Neilston station (not that Deepwood would be any better). Although, he supposed he could look forward to creature comforts like a television and a games console, which had been added to the cells in recent years - a move which many, including Pommery himself, had vehemently scorned. Anyway, they were getting rid of him today and that was all that mattered. He would contact the Procurator Fiscal after the arraignment and mention what Mert Irmak had told him about the prints in the vehicle and how they could still belong to Kieran Doyle, despite them not being able to obtain an exact match. Pommery had built a good relationship with the guys over at the PFs office on Ballater Street and he knew they would take care of it a lot better than he could.

The thirty-minute journey through to Glasgow was surprisingly quick, considering the usual Monday morning traffic. The three men in the car had all remained pretty much silent, with the exception of an occasional humming from the back. The plan was to drive into the gated area at the rear of the court building and transfer custody of Mr Doyle over to the bailiffs, who would escort him to the holding cells below ground, until it was his turn to appear before the Sheriff. All being well, Doyle would get an early slot on the day's roster and Officer Ward and he could be back on their way to Neilston by lunchtime. Unfortunately, for him and for everyone, this wasn't the way it had panned out.

***

The High Court of Justiciary in Glasgow is the supreme criminal court in Scotland. It sits in the

Saltmarket facing the McLennan Arch at the entrance
to Glasgow Green. On a sunny day like today, the
streets around the courthouse would likely be
crowded with people out making the most of the
weather, on their way to the park or into the city centre
to find a beer garden that had an empty table or a
bench that they could perch on and enjoy a cold drink.
The murder that had taken place in Neilston had not
yet reached the national press, so Pommery wasn't
expecting there to be any interference from the media,
which made his job a lot easier. The days of high-
profile murder trials in Scotland had peaked in the 80s
with the Ice Cream Wars. Since then, nothing seemed
to have piqued the media's interest with such ferocity.

The sun continued to beat down on the three men
in the police van as they approached the city centre.
Pommery hadn't checked, but he would guess the
temperature was hovering in the mid-twenties; a rare
and often capitalised on opportunity for the residents
of Glasgow. Especially after the months of continuous
rain that had percolated late summer.

They passed through the Gorbals and the
Riverside Campus of the City of Glasgow College, then
over the Albert Bridge that traversed the river Clyde,
towards the High Court of Justiciary building on the
far bank of the river. The sunlight sparkled on the
water like effervescent crystals on a sapphire blue
sports drink.

Officer Ward donned his sunglasses to counteract
the glare as they stepped out of the vehicle and into
the glorious saffron sun. Pommery grimaced when he
saw him, but secretly wished that he'd brought his

own pair of sunglasses as the daylight was blinding
him.

The small parking bay towards the rear of the
building was enclosed within a twenty-foot wall
topped with barbed wire and conspicuously placed
spikes for the pigeons. It was a mini fortress in the
heart of the city centre and just as well, Pommery
acknowledged. The High Court of Justiciary was
reserved for only the most despicable of cases.
Murderers, rapists, terrorists and paedophiles; this was
the clientele that frequented this building.

Ward approached the rear and unlocked the hold
with the key Pommery had entrusted to him. Kieran
Doyle sat smirking on the small metal bench; hands
cuffed between his knees and shoulders hunched
forwards.

'Comfortable?' Ward asked, as he leaned into the
hold and unlocked Doyle's cuffs from the bench they'd
been fastened to.

'Surprisingly so,' Doyle replied, letting his arms
stretch out in front of him.

'Your solicitor should be waiting for you inside,'
Ward continued, ignoring him.

'I know,' Doyle replied. 'I'm not paying him to sit
on his arse all day.'

'Well, for your sake, I hope you got a good one.'
He swung open the van doors, allowing Doyle to step
out into the sunlight. As he did so, Ward heard a loud
snap from behind him. Then another. He hadn't
realised what was happening until he saw Kieran
Doyle slump forward on the tarmac, his face a perfect
picture of pain.

'Shots fired!' Ward screamed, pulling the Glock 17 from his holster and swinging it in the direction of the court building.

Pommery was by his side in an instant, his own gun levelled out in front of him. 'Where?!' He bellowed, seeing the crumpled form beside the van.

'There! By the gates!' Ward had taken up position behind the van's open door and was peering out from behind it; his Glock pointed directly towards the point where he'd heard the gunfire.

Chapter 38
The Gunman

Noah Becker had made the decision to fire as soon as he'd seen the man's face. He crept silently behind the police van as it tittered between the gates and now lay crouched against the brick wall near the rear entrance to the court building. His Remington 700 hunting rifle, that he'd retrieved from the house in Neilston, was held firmly against his chest - he'd never used it for hunting anything other than pheasants before. He was all but certain that he'd hit the man clear through the chest with his second shot, but he could see that he was still squirming and knew that there was work still to be done. With the element of surprise gone, he would need to risk his cover in order to squeeze off one last round, and see the job done.

Chapter 39
Black Treacle

As the backdoor to the courthouse spilled open and frantic prison guards and bailiffs rushed towards the scene, Ward spotted movement by the west side of the building. He nudged the Chief with his elbow. 'He's over there,' he said, motioning to the far end of the car park.

Ward's outstretched hands were shaking. He squeezed them tightly around the handgrip, with his index finger levied over the trigger. Although he'd never discharged his service weapon in active duty before, he had trained for this moment for years, and he wouldn't be letting shaky hands get the better of him.

As the barrel of Noah Becker's rifle crept slowly out into the open, followed by the right side of his head, with the scope pressed firmly into socket of his right eye, he saw his shot and he took it. Another bullwhip snap echoed around the car park. Kieran Doyle, who had been writhing on the tarmac, jolted violently as the bullet pierced his abdomen. He lay still now, the life gone from behind his eyes. At the exact same instant, Officer Luke Ward caught the gleam from the scope of the shooters rifle. He raised his Glock and fired two clean shots across the tarmac. The first one hit the wall beside Becker's head; shards of brick shattered into the air. The second shot hit home, catching Noah Becker slightly below the clavicle, puncturing his right lung and knocking the air clean out of him. He slumped against the wall as the blood began to spill down his arm and trickle out onto the tarmac. The little pool of blood forming around his hand looked like black treacle melting in the brilliant yellow sun.

Chapter 40
Rolling Heads

Bill Pommery thrust his hands deep into the warm soil, held the head at the base and used his knife to severe it clean. He threw it to one side, next to the growing pile of rolling heads behind him. Harvesting the cabbages was the last of the chores that he'd assigned himself to do on this wonderfully hot Sunday morning. On his wife's urging, he'd decided to take the afternoon off, and he was looking forward to enjoying a cold beer in the garden once the vegetable patch was seen to.

It had been nearly a month since the incident behind the High Court of Justiciary building in Glasgow. Both Kieran Doyle and Noah Becker were now buried alongside their respective families in Neilston Cemetery. It had been hard going for a while in the weeks following the incident, but he sensed that things were now finally starting to get back to normal. He'd had an interview with Superintendent Rutherford and Chief Constable Alan Cummings the previous week, to go over his version of the events. As a key witness, his testimony had been crucial in the official documenting of events. Before the meeting, he had the funny feeling that heads were about to roll.

In the end, as was expected by nearly everybody, Officer Ward's swift actions were deemed lawful, proportionate and necessary at the time, and he was commended for his bravery and promoted to the position of Sergeant. If he hadn't acted so instinctively, then who knows what more damage the lone shooter could have caused. Two court bailiffs and a correctional officer had spilled out onto the scene at the sounds of gunfire. More lives could've been lost, but thankfully they weren't thanks to the young Sergeant's heroics.

The day following his interview, Pommery had tended his resignation to Superintendent Rutherford. He was now looking forward to winding down his last few months on the force before finally retiring. It was time, he sensed, and Mandy wholeheartedly agreed with him. Nothing quite awakens you to the transience of your own mortality that being fired at by a gunman with nothing left to lose.

He'd had plenty of time to ponder what really happened that day - the significance had not been lost on him as it was on others. The final showdown in the carpark hadn't just been between Kieran Doyle and Noah Becker, but between the last remaining combatants in the Becker and Doyle households. The two families had essentially wiped each other out (or cancelled each other out; however you wanted to look at it). It was almost Shakespearean in a sense. Beckers' and Doyles'. Montagues' and Capulets'.

For those of a Shakespearean persuasion, they might even argue that the incident was reminiscent of the scene in *Romeo and Juliet*, where Romeo kills Tybalt, or Tybalt kills Mercutio, or one of those scenes (Bill was no expert). He'd looked up the excerpt on the internet one day.

> *Two households, both alike in dignity,*
> *In fair Verona, where we lay our scene,*
> *From ancient grudge break to new mutiny,*
> *Where civil blood makes civil hands unclean.*
> *From forth the fatal loins of these two foes*
> *A pair of star-cross'd lovers take their life.*

He supposed it was fitting in a loose sort of way - although the only instance of star-crossed lovers had been incestuous (the artefacts from the macabre shrine found in the Grey's farm were still held in evidence at the station). He'd received curious news from the Procurator Fiscal's office the previous week regarding Mr Doyle. They had conducted a thorough background check on the young man and some interesting things had come to light. They confirmed that he'd been working on an oil rig in the North Sea for nearly the past decade, ending in the spring of this year (so he can't have been squatting at the Grey's farm for longer than a few months). Also, and most peculiarly of all, his superiors aboard the rig had had some strange things to say about Mr Doyle's behaviour. It seemed at times he was unable to tell where he was – specifically, he was never quite sure if he were on land or at sea. From all out outwardly accounts it appeared the young man had been highly delusional, to say the least.

Strangely, the DNA that was found belonging to Mr Doyle at the crime scene was confirmed to be much fresher than they had originally suspected. Meaning that he'd potentially revisited the crime scene on several occasions after the murder. Anyway, all of that was now in the past.

Bill tossed the last head of cabbage on the grass beside him and wiped the dripping sweat from his brow. It'd been some month, but now it was over. Mandy arrived by his side, bent down and kissed him on his dirt-mottled cheek. In her hands she had two ice-cold bottles of Corona; she held one against his cheek and he sighed in satisfaction as the icy glass touched his skin.

'Thought you could use a drink,' she said, kneeling down beside him.

'You thought right.' He reached over and kissed her on the lips, then took a long gratifying gulp from his bottle. He had the funny feeling that heads were about to roll; but only the ones he used for making sauerkraut.

Epilogue
Adam Hunt

Adam Hunt awoke in the same soiled sheets he'd
spent the last month sleeping in. The morning wakeup
call wasn't for another twenty minutes - his body clock
had just started to adjust to work in tandem with the
stringent prison routine.

The monotony of each day inside was not
something that bothered him. The routine kept him
ordered and sane. Without it, prison life would quickly
unravel into an unimaginable hell. Order keeps the
wheels-a-turnin' and keeps the incarcerated man from
descending into madness.

His cell mate was still sleeping. A fat loathsome
fellow, who smoked more than a chimney on a turn of
the century factory. He coughed loudly in his sleep
then rolled over onto his belly, causing the bed springs
to reel and pang in a clackity clang of protest.

He kicked his legs over the side of the bed and
stretched his toes out on the floor. Today was his one-
month anniversary of being inside. One down and 215
more to go. But it wasn't good to be keeping track of
time like that (outside the hours in the day that is).

When you started ticking off the weeks and the months, the true enormity of the time you have left hits you like a rusty blade through your innards.

The letters he'd received the previous week were still tucked neatly between the bed springs above him. The first letter had been from the SPS (Scottish Prison Service). They had written to inform him that two of his estranged relatives had met their untimely ends in remarkably close proximity. His aunt Gwen and his cousin Claire, both dead - or so the SPS said.

He'd received further word from his father in a follow-up letter that'd gone into more of the specifics. His cousin had been killed in a car accident, not too far south of where he was sitting - coincidence? He thought it unlikely. And his aunt - he could barely believe what he was reading - was the victim of a suspected murder.

Then, to add another bizarre twist to this tale, he'd received a third letter from the SPS which informed him of the death of his other cousin, Noah. He was anxiously awaiting the follow-up letter from his father to elaborate on the matter.

He reached under the springs and pulled out the second letter (the one from his father), that was stained with ink blots and written in an almost illegible scrawl - although the language was remarkably concise.

Adam,

I hope you are well. I realise we haven't spoken much over the past couple of years and this is something I deeply regret.

I know you were once close to your aunt Gwendolyn and uncle Frank, so I feel compelled to write to you to tell you that both Gwen and your cousin Claire have sadly passed away in the past couple of days.

Claire was involved in a car accident near Pitlochry (I suspect she may have been on her way to see you at the time).

I feel especially saddened by this as I also suspect that I may have been one of the last people on Earth to see her alive. During her visit, Claire informed me that she suspected her mother had been murdered and this was no doubt on her mind at the time of the accident. I realise this is painful news to be getting, especially in your current situation, but I thought it best that you know, as the two of you were once close.

I've enclosed a stamped envelope, should you wish to write back.

Jack.

Adam re-folded the letter and stashed it in the bedsprings above him. He couldn't help but feel curious about the circumstances surrounding his aunt's death in particular. His uncle and his own mother (siblings) had both died within a short space of time, and he couldn't help but sense a form of deja vu emerging with this new spat of deaths in the family. It seemed that as a family they were cursed.

It was true, he had once been close to his cousin Claire when they were young, but not anymore. Those days were cemented firmly in the past. He used to be able to tell her anything that was on his mind. Any secret thing that he hadn't told anyone, he always found he could confide it in her. That wouldn't be the case anymore. For instance, he would never confide in her the fact that his wife had been cheating on him with a man she'd met at work, and he'd never confide in her the fact that he'd been so embarrassed by this betrayal that he'd taken the knife from the rack beside the kettle and thrust into her neck, as she made her way across the living room to fetch them some wine. These were things he couldn't have confided in Claire anymore. She was a stranger to him. And now she was a dead stranger.

Adam thought it curious that his father should mention that he was one of the last people on Earth to see Claire before she died. Perhaps he'd known why she'd come... Perhaps she'd asked him awkward questions... Incriminating questions... Perhaps he'd slipped something in her drink when she wasn't looking. Nobody would know except him...

It'd occurred to him over the years that if he'd wanted to, his father could have easily meddled with his mother's prescriptions, making her death look like an accident or suicide. Was it coincidence that he'd been the last person on Earth to see both of these women alive? He was the common denominator, there was no denying that. Perhaps, he was responsible for the deaths of them both? He could never know for sure. He'd been suspicious of his father ever since he'd found that old licence plate lying next to a can of red spray-paint, tucked away in the attic.

Anyway, if that was in fact the case, like father like son, he supposed...